Home to Home

Home to Home

Understanding the Family

MICHAEL MOYNAGH

daybreak
London

First published in 1990 by
Daybreak
Darton, Longman and Todd Ltd
89 Lillie Road, London SW6 1UD

© 1990 Michael Moynagh

British Library Cataloguing in Publication Data
Moynagh, Michael
  Home to home
  1. Families. Social aspects – Christian viewpoints
  I. Title
  261.83585

ISBN 0–232–51854–8

The scriptural quotations are taken from
the New International Version of the Bible
published by Hodder and Stoughton Ltd

Phototypeset by Input Typesetting Ltd
London SW19 8DR
Printed and bound in Great Britain by
Courier International Ltd, Tiptree, Essex

Contents

Acknowledgements	vi
Introduction: Setting out	1

PART ONE Harmful families

1 Hurt by their society	9
2 Hurt by their history	18
3 Hurt by their morality	27

PART TWO Envisioned families

4 Spreading out	41
5 Passing on	51
6 Shining through	63

PART THREE Enabled families

7 Family despair	77
8 Family deliverance	87
9 Family destination	97

PART FOUR Enthused families

10 Extended out	109
11 Handed on	116
12 Reflected back	126

PART FIVE Hopeful families

13 Healing values	139
14 Healing the past	148
15 Healing society	158
16 Another view of family	167
Bibliography	177

Acknowledgements

Home to Home started life while I was studying in the Theology Department at Bristol University. I am very grateful to Dr Denys Turner for his early help and encouragement, and also to Mr Philip Kingston in the Department of Social Work. The Vicar, the Revd Derek Osborne, kindly gave me time off to write while I was on the staff of Emmanuel Church, Northwood. I benefited immensely from the comments of those who read early drafts of the book – the Revd Dr David Atkinson, the Revd Francis Palmer, Mr Philip Sampson, the Revd Sue Walrond-Skinner and Mrs Jean Watson. The remaining defects are mine. I am specially grateful for all that I learnt at Emmanuel, during which time the bulk of the book was written, and for my experience of love at Wilton where the book was completed. My best teacher and source of love has been my wife, Liz, and our two children, Felicity and Simon. To them the book is dedicated.

Introduction: Setting out

At the end of my first job as a clergyman, someone remarked that Liz and I had produced a family that had been a good example to the parish. Liz and I laughed afterwards as we thought, 'Little do they know!' There must be many families like ours which look fine one moment but are full of heartaches the next, and which long for something better.

This book is written for all those who are interested in families – for befrienders and visitors who have had no training at all, for professional carers, for clergy, for those who are intrigued by their families and for all who long for more loving homes.

There are so many books on the family that I balk at adding to the pile. Christians seem to devour them by the dozen! Many of them are 'hints and tips' books which are easy to read and sometimes rather good. Others are more profound (and often more dull), looking at families from a psychological or sociological perspective.

And then there are books which relate the Christian faith to particular issues like divorce, abortion and the role of women. Remarkably few, however, provide an overview of biblical teaching about families. Hence this particular book. Its focus is on how Scripture can help us not only to survive families, but enjoy them.

Liberated families

This approach is different to the traditional, humpty-dumpty defense of the family, which says that the family has had a great fall and needs the bits stuck together again. Traditionalists attack those whom they believe gave the family the big shove – feminists for example, those in the media and the schools who have preached a false view of family life, and governments which have pursued policies that have weakened the family. They want to persuade the public that the family is a Good Thing and that it needs to be defended urgently.[1]

This view recognises the fun and laughter that can go on at home; it underlines how children can grow into emotionally healthy adults when they are given a sense of security, value and meaning by their parents; it remembers those parents who spend hours encouraging their children to learn a valued skill – the professional musician, perhaps, who owes everything to the support he or she got from home.

But there is an unreality about it. At times it almost idolises the family. It tries to convince people of something they already know. For if you went into a shopping precinct and asked people if they thought the family was a good thing, virtually everyone would reply 'Yes!' One survey found that ninety-one per cent of fifteen to nineteen-year-olds expect to marry, and sixty-seven per cent expect their marriage to last till death. The overwhelming majority expect to have children. Half of those who divorce think marriage is sufficiently worthwhile to try again.[2]

Top of the domestic agenda today is not whether the family is a good idea, but how it can live up to the high expectations people have of it. With one in two new marriages in the United States ending in divorce, and one in three in Britain, family life is clearly not what people hope it to be. They feel unfairly treated by their spouses – or by their children, or by their parents. That is what matters to most people, not whether the idea of family needs defending.

At the other extreme are the radical critics of the family. In the late 1960s and early 1970s the British psychiatrists, R. D. Laing and David Cooper, launched a blistering attack on the family. They accused it of suffocating the individual by enmeshing him in a web of family rules. Particularly vicious, they said, were rules which trapped a family member so that whatever she did she would always be blamed for getting it wrong. If she kept quiet she would be criticised for not joining in, but if she spoke up she would be blamed for interrupting the adults.

1. E.g. Digby Anderson and Graham Dawson (eds.), *Family Portraits*.
2. Andrew Graystone, 'Dynamics of family', unpublished paper.

INTRODUCTION: SETTING OUT

Each person according to Laing and Cooper has a mental picture of what they want the others in the family to be. The strongest in the family are able to impose their picture on the others by 'writing' the family's rules. Weaker members, forced to conform to the image, are prevented from becoming properly themselves. Often a person might be required to be several different, contradictory people at the same time, and to split himself up. He may conform to Dad's picture of him one moment, and Mum's the next. If both parents are in the room, he may try to split himself between the two.

Struck by the injustices of family life, Cooper in particular called for the abolition of the family and its replacement by less oppressive communes. Though since the mid 1970s few people have been as wholesale in their attack on the family, nearly a decade later Laing was still as trenchant in his views. He talked about the 'normal' families he had researched and how 'stifling and deadening' they seemed. They appeared to differ from schizophrenic families only in that no one cracked up.[3]

Similar attacks have been made on the family by radical feminists. They have condemned it for producing stereotyped gender roles. Parents have particular expectations of how girls should behave, and they pass those expectations on by rewarding the girl, for example, with a smile when she gets out her doll. The child is prevented from realising her full potential because her so-called 'masculine' traits are stereotyped as masculine, and so are never drawn out.[4]

These broadsides are an improvement on the stick-the-family-together-again approach because they take seriously injustice within the family. But they provide no real solution. By and large, the communes that were tried in the 1960s and 1970s were not a success. Many suffered from an instability which denied children the security they need; they failed to create communities where members genuinely accepted each other; they had very limited success in freeing their members from the traditional gender roles imposed by their families. Even their supporters had to admit that the experiments failed.

---

3. David Cooper, *The Death of the Family*; R. D. Laing, *The Politics of the Family*; Richard Simon, 'Still R. D. Laing after all these years', pp. 23–61.

4. Lynne Segal (ed.), *What is to be done about the family?*

The task of overcoming the damaging side of family life remained.[5]

There is a third approach to the family which avoids the naive adulation of the first and the deep hostility of the second. It recognises both the shortcomings of the family, and its potential to bring out the best in its members. It shows how the family can struggle against the harmful tendencies which its critics highlight, so that its potential for good – which its traditional supporters underline – can be more fully realised.

George Bernard Shaw once said, 'We spend the first half of our lives enduring our parents, and the second half enduring our children.' This third approach says that there is no need for families to settle for a life of endurance: they can be freed from many of their limitations.

It's inevitable that a book about the family will focus on the family, and perhaps it is also inevitable that this could be easily misunderstood. We shall be showing how families can respond to the world, and this could be taken to imply that families are the most important institution in society – that if we get the family right everything else will come right too. But that's not the basic argument of this book. Certainly we shall have many reminders of the importance of the family. Yet there are other aspects of society – the employment market, government, business and so on – which are at least equally, if not more important. Indeed, to understand fully what is happening to families, these other dimensions need to be studied as well.

But what is the family?

So much ink has been spilt trying to answer that, and with such meagre results, that we shall not spend long on it here. The problem arises because it is so hard to find a definition which embraces the western nuclear family, the African extended family, gay marriages and heterosexual marriages, single-parent families and so on.

Part of the problem is that modern society has tended to narrow down the boundaries of the family to the 'ideal' nuclear

---

5. Wendy Clark, 'Home Thoughts from Not So Far Away: A Personal Look at Family' in Lynne Segal (ed.), *op. cit*, pp. 168–9; Mica Nava, 'From Utopianism to Scientific Feminism? Early Feminist Critiques of the Family', in Lynne Segal (ed.), *op. cit*, pp. 67–8.

family of certain TV commercials. Yet Scripture, by contrast, keeps pushing out the boundaries of the family. The Old Testament word for family (*mishpaha*), for instance, is a fluid term blurring distinctions between family and tribe, and family and nation. The term for house, *beth*, is also fluid. It may refer to the smallest family unit, the clan, or to the entire nation (the 'house of Israel').

We shall see how in Scripture family can extend to distant relatives, to those who belong to God's family, and to those outside God's family waiting to be drawn in. It is almost as broad as you care to make it. So when the next chapters talk about families in their modern, narrower and exclusive sense, perhaps it would be as well to keep in mind that the Bible has a much wider and all-embracing vision.

PART ONE
Harmful families

1

Hurt by their society

James was a consultant at a teaching hospital, and he had a large private practice. He drew a good income, and was highly regarded. The hospital porters, nurses, junior doctors and registrars all looked up to him, and so did people outside the profession. His life had a purpose – he saw hundreds of patients each year. His research had yielded significant results, which gave him a sense of achievement. He could interpret his life since school as a series of steps up the professional ladder. He had too a sense of belonging – to a hospital community and a professional one. No wonder that work was tremendously important.

What a contrast to his family! Despite all that the family could give him – sexual fulfilment, intimacy and the joy of parenthood, for example – James got no income from home (his wife earned a little, but not much). There was little prestige in being a father – millions become fathers: there are not many hospital consultants. Though James was proud of his children, he only had two. Hundreds of patients seemed far more important. His research was acclaimed by colleagues all over the world, but only his wife and children recognised his successes at home. (And if James was honest, these successes were at least equalled by his failures.)

The landmarks of passing key exams, getting that senior registrar's post and then landing a plum consultant's job loomed larger in James's memory than some of the family milestones (though he could still remember his wedding anniversary!). There was a feeling of belonging at home, but it was to a smaller and less prestigious community.

Perhaps this is an extreme example, though similar things could be said of other professions and of many successful businessmen. Yet it illustrates how work has pushed the family to the edge of many people's lives. It is one of the social pressures which hurt families, so that families become hurtful themselves. In this chapter we shall be looking at some of these pressures (there isn't space to look at them all), and then in the next two chapters we shall consider some of the psychological and moral pressures.

Families on the edge

Work pushed family to the edge of James's life because he got more income, social status, purpose, achievement, a more significant framework for interpreting his life and a greater sense of belonging from his career than from home. Not everyone is as fortunate, in career terms, as James. But a hospital porter would find that the bulk of his family income came from his job, he would have a certain status (as the family breadwinner), his job would be a reason to get up in the morning, he might have a feeling of achievement from a good day's work, and he would belong to a group of workmates and to a hospital community.

The sidelining of families by work owes much to the way that work has been hived off from home over the past 250 years. Up to the mid-eighteenth century work used to reinforce family ties. The whole family might help on the land. It was as much a work unit as a family unit. Industrialisation led to the separation of work from home, and to the artificial distinction between 'productive work' which was paid and 'non-productive', unpaid work in the family. Work which received wages became more highly valued than housework which did not.

Because work was some distance from home it developed its own community, and its rewards of success, status and so on were earned away from the family. These rewards became so highly prized that steadily more women have left home in search of them. Housework has come to appear positively dull by comparison.

Not everyone realises what huge effects the separation of work from home in the last century had on the family. It meant that an increasing number of mothers spent more time with their children. Before the industrial revolution it seems that they left their babies swaddled and unattended for long periods as they helped on the farm, or (with families literally the fabric of society) as they spun and weaved in the house.

During the nineteenth and early twentieth centuries, first the rich and then gradually working-class mothers became full-time mums, which meant that they drew emotionally much closer to their children. They spent more time with them. This gave mothers who were temperamentally inclined more opportunity to smother their children emotionally, to invade their privacy and to cling anxiously to them, making them insecure.

Maria for example was a real worry-er. From the moment her daughter was born, she was frightened she would have a cot death, or that she would fall and hurt herself as she was learning to walk, or that she would get run over as she walked to school. The worry was never-ending. Maria was at home all day, which meant that the little girl could never escape her mum's anxiety. She grew into a timid and nervous adult. Injustice was done – unintentionally – because the child was never given the confidence to become fully herself.

Two hundred and fifty years ago Maria would have swaddled her baby and left her for most of the day. Her husband would have been around more to temper Maria's nervousness. From the age of seven or eight there was a good chance the young girl would have escaped her mother's worry by working as a servant in another house. (During the eighteenth century, nearly half the adolescents worked as an apprentice or a servant away from home.) The daughter would have been less affected by her mother's anxiety.

The split between work and home has also produced the more familiar 'absentee father' syndrome. If the father is not physically away working or travelling, frequently his job leaves him so exhausted that he has little emotional energy for the home. If the mother is working as well, the problem can be even worse. Many a family has become a collection of individuals sharing the same roof and the same TV, but living as 'intimate strangers' to each other. The children feel unfairly neglected and of marginal importance.

Women on the edge

In her picture of *The Family* Paula Rego, an acclaimed artist whose recent paintings have been described by Germaine Greer as 'undeniably, obviously, triumphantly female', portrays an ineffectual man sitting weakly at the foot of a bed. Mother and daughter womanhandle him by tugging at his clothes. With mother's arm wrenching his face backward as she hauls at his sleeves, it is plain that the man is being stifled. A little girl stands menacingly, back to the window, and stares approvingly at what is going on.

The heroines have old-fashioned, distinctly female clothes; mother has a bow in her hair. The furniture also reflects a bygone age – a water-jug suggests an era before running water. The message is very direct. Women from traditional homes – oppressed women it is implied – are fighting back. The tables have been turned, and the women are bristling with vengeance. Families which push women to the edge reap their rewards in female nastiness.

Some people would say that women have been pushed to the edge of the family, in terms of status, by the family itself. The way children are brought up leads to an expectation that men's interests are more important than women's, and this influences adult behaviour. Others would say that male dominance is so built into society that families can scarcely escape its influence. The pressure is from society more than the home. This is a chicken and egg question which illustrates how the family both influences society and is influenced by it.

What is clear is that social developments over the past 200 years have increased the pressure on families to treat women unfairly. The subordinate position of women was reinforced by the separation of paid work from the home. Wives became wholly dependent on the man financially, whereas before – through their household cottage industries and their work on the farm – they had been economically important to their husbands.

The male 'macho' image was reinforced in the last century by the physical brutality of many jobs. By contrast the mother, with her child-rearing responsibilities, was expected increasingly to display a softer, more caring approach. It seemed so 'natural' for the man to sit at the head of the table and take the key decisions. He was the one on whom the family economically depended. It was his interests which the wife lovingly and unstintingly served. 'I gave him the best years of my life. . .', she may later recall, perhaps with a tinge of regret.

The growing number of women in paid work since the war,

which has made them financially more independent of their husbands, and the feminist movement (among other things) have led to a huge change in expectations. Husbands and wives have been encouraged to see themselves as equal partners and to be more flexible in their roles. Yet the woman's interests still tend to be secondary to the man's. When it comes to the decision whether to move, for example, the husband's job even now will often have priority over his wife's.

It seems that wives in full and part-time work still do the bulk of the shopping and most of the domestic chores. One study found that of those in full-time jobs, men have about twenty and a half hours of free time each weekend, against fourteen and a half for women. Wives tend to be mainly or solely responsible for three-quarters of the housework, while men do over eighty per cent of the repairs (which are often more interesting).[1] Traditional roles need not be unfair if both partners have an equal say in the decision. The trouble is that roles are frequently chosen with the interests of the husband chiefly in mind.

The burden on women is likely to increase. The number of ageing people in the West is multiplying dramatically. Between 1985 and the year 2000, the number of pensioners in Britain is expected to grow by 50 per cent. The elderly frequently require much care and time, and women in particular are expected to provide that support. In many countries governments are actively encouraging the elderly to be looked after at home, which in practice usually means by women. If the woman has a paid job as well, her workload is likely to be extremely heavy, and the division of labour in the family to be even more unfair. Home will become a workhouse.[2]

Marital relationships, like political ones, can be based on power, and often involve a battle for the control of key resources, for better opportunities and for the support of others. Husband and wife tussle over who is going to make the decisions, how the chores are to be divided and who is going to get the better deal. The children are enlisted on either side.

Feminists complain that in this struggle the change in expectations has not gone far enough, the interests of the man still

---

1. Melanie Henwood, Lesley Rimmer and Malcolm Wicks, *Inside the Family: Changing Roles of Men and Women*, pp. 66–7.

2. Diana Guttins, *The Family in Question: Changing Households and Familiar Ideologies*, p. 10.

come first, roles are still stereotyped, many women are sexually and physically abused, and mothers who want to work cannot do so because there are no child-care facilities – that justice has yet to be done.

On the edge of community

Families are rather like a pond which dries up if no water flows in. Their emotional reserves evaporate unless they are renewed by the support of other people. The mother who is exhausted from paid work and has no one to turn to at weekends will lack the energy to be patient with her children, let alone play with them. The children will be screamed at one moment and indulged the next.

Many parents are in that position, a long way from relatives and alone in their neighbourhood. It is often thought that this is quite a recent problem – that there used to be a golden age of the extended family, supported by a stable network of village relationships. Friends and relatives were close by to lend mothers a hand. The industrial revolution, it is said, brought this period largely to an end.

'Not so!' say many experts. In northern Europe and North America the extended family hardly existed and village life was not particularly stable: people moved a lot. The historian, Peter Laslett, has found that the average size of British households was much the same before 1800 as it is now. Many more children were born, but many more died. That was so much a fact of life that it was not unknown for parents, expecting one of the children to die, to give two of them the same name.[3]

It was no more common to find homes with grandparents, parents and children under the same roof before the industrial revolution than it is today. Often relatives lived nearer to each other. But people travelled by foot or horse-drawn carriage, which meant that it could take as long to go five miles then as it does to drive eighty miles now. Postal services were notoriously unreliable, and there was no telephone! Greater ease of communication may well mean that modern families have more contact with their members than their predecessors a century or more ago.

3. Peter Laslett, *Household and Family in Past Time*, pp. 57–67.

Though travel was slow, it seems to have been quite common for people to live away from their home village or town. This was especially true during the industrial revolution. In the early nineteenth century, well over half the British population were not living in the place where they were born. The lonely family, deprived of the support of relatives and friends, the victim of mobility, seems not to be such a modern phenomenon. It may well have always existed.[4]

Whether the isolated family is a new problem or not, it is certainly a major one. Many couples are uprooted by companies, property developers and by the destruction of local jobs. Cut off from the affirmation of friends and relatives, spouses lack the emotional reserves to build each other up. Fragile inside, they hit out at the other's self-esteem – and at the children too.

The US Army recently researched the high divorce rate among its members. Most divorces and other marital problems were found to be caused by the constant uprooting of families. Wives were perpetually being hauled out of networks of friends and neighbours. The marriage alone was left to sustain that sense of well-being which should have been rooted in a wider community. Often it could not take the strain. It was being asked to carry too much. The army promptly adopted a policy of lower mobility.[5]

On the edge of prosperity

A British study of teen-age mothers found that only a quarter actually planned to get pregnant. Many of the girls had deliberately given up contraception while denying any desire to have a baby. They made remarks like, 'I didn't like taking the pill', and 'My boyfriend hid them'.

The researcher, Dr Ineichen, suspected that the real reason was that these premature mums had fatalistic perceptions of themselves and their future. They were all working class, many had been unemployed. Their lives seemed to be going nowhere. Motherhood offered a way out – a route to adult status.

---

4. J. E. Goldthorpe, *Family Life in Western Societies: A Historical Sociology of Family Relationships in Britain and North America*. CUP 1987, pp. 1–40.
5. *Family Base News* 1988.

Children became a social analgesic to deaden the pain of poverty and powerlessness.[6]

Yet children brought up in poverty are more likely than their middle-class peers to experience acute family stress. Research shows that the great majority of children entering care at a young age come from chronically deprived families facing crisis situations. Summarising this research, Robert Holman, the author of a classic book on the subject, wrote that the pressures on poor families are so great 'that it is surprising that so many of the poor survive and still maintain their family units.'[7]

Poor families are more likely than others to be badly fed and to suffer from ill-health. If Mum is in and out of hospital and Dad is on shift work, it is a safe bet that the children will be neglected. Poor families tend to live in cramped conditions, which means that peace with the neighbours usually comes before the needs of the children. Normally they can't afford outings, books and educational toys which stimulate a child's intellectual development.

Parents in poverty frequently lose their self-respect and develop a negative self-image. Father will feel a failure if he cannot give his children as many presents as their friends get, or if he is unable to repay treats given to his children by their friends' parents.

Parents may feel they have failed because they have had to lower their expectations. One study of slum families found that parents did share the values of middle-class parents in wanting their children to succeed, be honest and reliable, and so on. But poverty forced them to lower their sights, make do with second-best and spend less time with their children.

All this can lead to prolonged feelings of inferiority. These feelings may come out in aggression, an heroic lashing out to assert oneself and show that the ego has not been crushed, but which leaves the children emotionally and perhaps physically scarred. Or they can lead to withdrawal. Parents may seek to avoid the reality of apparent failure by apathy (so that they do not provide for their children), by an unwillingness to be helped (which would be admitting that they can't cope), or by alcohol (which deadens their awareness). The children are not given a fair chance.

6. Bernard Ineichen, *Journal of Biosocial Science*, vol. 18, no. 4, 1987, 387.
7. Robert Holman, *Inequality in Child Care*. Child Poverty Action Group, London 1980, p. 16.

'I sort of gave up', said one mother who was haggling with the social security officers, 'because no matter who you turn to they say it's not my problem – I'll send you to so and so. Well, when you've got two young babies and you've got to trek say half-way across the borough to find this bloke who's going to help you, see this person here and that person somewhere else, and then when you get there they're not in or they can't do anything about it. You just stop dead, and you're pretty run down anyway and you think, "This is not worth it".'[8] Children on the edge of prosperity – close to it but unable to reach it – often feel 'not worth it'.

There are other social pressures on the family of course – the tendency for people to live longer for example, which means more older relatives for families to look after and longer marriages. If a couple stays together till death, the partners are likely to have to come to terms with far more changes in each other than would have been the case when people died younger.

Yet among the main pressures are that families are left on the edge of work, and the rights of wives are pushed to the edge of marital horizons. Many families are alone, on the edge of community. Poor families are on the edge of prosperity. These pressures provoke damaging responses at home which put members of the family on edge.

---

8. Peter Beresford, John Kenmis, Jane Tunstill, *In Care in North Battersea*, p. 18.

2

Hurt by their history

The British Labour politician, Roy Hattersley, was brought up in a Yorkshire working-class family which was dominated by his mother. As a boy during the Second World War, he idolised General Wavell who was serving with the British forces in North Africa. He remembers:

> One day, I took a piece of flat sandstone that had been unearthed in the churchyard and – copying the work of stonemasons whom I had often watched as they added a name to a tombstone – I carved 'WAVELL' on it. When I had propped it up in the little strip of sunless garden in the shadow of the churchyard wall which was said to be mine, I called my mother to marvel at my handiwork.
>
> She was furious. For us, there was only one hero in North Africa. So I took the old skrew-driver that I had used as a chisel and inscribed SYD [his uncle] on the other side. My mother helped to embed it in *her* rockery. I had learned another lesson about the rigid rules of our closely-knit community.[1]

Every family has its rules. Some are obvious. Sunday lunch is always at 1.00 p.m. – exactly. The child who is late is welcomed with disapproval. Other rules are different because they contain an injunction that the rule is not to be discussed. Some families have a rule that there should be no disagreement. It is never spelt out, but – partly because it is hidden – it is very powerful.

So when disagreement brews an outsider might sense a general uneasiness, a heightening of tension in the room. Someone may try to change the subject. 'Where shall we walk this afternoon?' Mum unexpectedly asks her daughter, as it becomes obvious that Dad wants to go to Spain that summer while she

---

1. Roy Hattersley, *A Yorkshire Boyhood*. London 1981, p. 76.

wants to go to the South of France. Mum hopes the family will be distracted by deciding to go on their favourite walk. Or Dad will crack a joke, in the hope that family unity will break out as they laugh together. He knows that he is going to win the argument anyway, by booking the holiday when Mum's back is turned!

Some family rules, like mealtimes, are pretty innocuous. Some, such as the requirement that everyone helps with the chores, can be healthy. But others are unjust – they damage the interests of family members. A rule not to disagree can stifle the family. It can smother imagination by preventing someone exploring new ideas which the others may not like. In extreme cases it can prevent adolescents from becoming mature. They remain like Rosemary in Scott Fitzgerald's novel, *Tender is the Night*, who was always 'assuming the image of her mother, ever carried with her'.

There are scores of unjust rules: the 'rule' that everyone stops talking when Mum (but not Dad) begins to speak, that Dad needn't help in the kitchen because he can't cope even though he manages a factory perfectly well for the rest of the week, that the boys stick up for each other but not their sister, that the little boy holds his mother's hand in the park when he could run free, that Dad chooses what to watch on TV, and so on. The rules are unjust because the interests of one person are given undue weight, or because those of someone else suffer.

In the last chapter we saw how certain features of society encourage acts of injustice within the home. This chapter looks at why unjust rules persist within families – at why the past imperfect keeps making the present tense.

Don't expect to change

One reason why these unjust rules persist within families is the strong tendency for family rules to get passed on to the next generation. How this happens is a matter of debate. Some psychologists argue that young children identify with their parents. They try to see the world through their parents' eyes. Normally the boy will identify with his father, and the girl with her mother. Unconsciously the young boy wants to become like his father and so he copies him. When he becomes an adult, he finds himself imposing the same rules on his family as his father did at home.

Others say that little children recognise how their parents control key 'rewards' – food, special treats, fun and games, affection and so on. Their antennae pick up that certain forms of behaviour are rewarded, while others result in the rewards being withdrawn. The little girl spots that Dad will put his arm round her if she nestles up to him when he argues with Mum. Her mother makes no comment, which suggests that it is safe for the girl tacitly to side with her father in family rows. This becomes so much part of her life that she does not notice when, as a mother, she allows the same to happen in her family.

There is no need to see these as rival theories: they may well be complementary. They explain why people carry their family's rules into adulthood. But what happens when people marry? If a couple from similar families get together, it is easy to see how they will bring two similar sets of rules into their new home. It will resemble the households in which they were brought up. But what about opposites who pair up? Won't the fusion of two different sets of rules create a home that really is new?

Some experts would say that it is quite common for opposites to attract. But others argue that it is nearly always the case that people marry someone with similarities in their background. A couple may appear different superficially, but what draws them together is that beneath the surface their homes had important things in common. They are likely to have first recognised these similarities, while they were still strangers, by means of each other's body language.

So a woman may see a man whose posture, facial expressions and the typical way he moves betray deep-seated emotions. If he is a depressive, he will move apathetically and slump and slouch. The person whose hands are slightly tense will express some anxiety. These physical signs begin to tell the girl about the man's family.

If he was brought up in a household where love was seldom expressed openly, this will be reflected in mannerisms that will make him appear 'cold'. If his family was up front about their feelings of anger, then he will appear comfortable in a situation where conflict is brewing. His body-language will describe his family's rules for handling emotions.

Now it may be that these rules will have encouraged the man

to hide some of his feelings. Perhaps his family found it difficult to be open about sex. There was a rule that sex was not to be discussed. So the man hides his true feelings by talking about it at one remove: he laughs raucously at sexual jokes and tells them himself. And that becomes one of the reasons why the woman is attracted to him. She was brought up in a home that was embarrassed by sex too, but in her case she doesn't talk about it at all.

On the surface the two seem very different. He is quite extrovert and frequently laughs about sex. She is quieter and never speaks about it. But underneath they are similar. They have both been brought up in families where true feelings about sex were a particular cause of anxiety.

They meet in a pub where a number of the lads are exchanging dirty jokes. Their reactions betray the fact that they have this anxiety in common, making them feel safe in each other's company, and that becomes the starting-point of their relationship. Not surprisingly, the family they create will have a rule which says – once again – that sex is a cause for anxiety and feelings about it must be suppressed.

Robin Skynner and John Cleese, in their book on how to survive families, have described the Family Systems Exercise which is used in the training of family therapists. It demonstrates how in marriage like background almost always attracts like background. Trainees are brought together while they are still strangers, and asked to choose another person from the group. They must choose a person who makes them think of someone in their family, or who gives them the feeling that he or she would have filled a 'gap' in their family.

The trainees are not allowed to talk while making their choices. They just wander round looking at all the others. When they have chosen someone and then compared their family backgrounds, the couples are asked to select another pair to make foursomes. Each foursome is encouraged to form itself into a family of some kind, each person taking on a role within the family. Then they talk about what it was in their family backgrounds that led to their decisions, and report back to the wider group.

Invariably, what they find is that each person has picked out three people whose families functioned in very similar ways to their own. The families may have had difficulty sharing affection or expressing anger, there may have been near-incestuous relationships, all four fathers may have been away from home in the crucial early years, and so on.

Sometimes the exercise leaves two or three people on the edge of the group, who come together when all the others have paired up. What is particularly interesting is how they often discover that they had also been on the edge of the families into which they were born. They had been fostered, or adopted, or brought up in children's homes.[2]

The uncanny tendency for marriage partners to come from similar families means that the most powerful domestic rules will be passed from one generation to the next. For it was those rules which brought the spouses together in the first place. Less powerful rules, which may differ between the two homes, get handed on through a process of 'bargaining'. Some things will be done her way, and others his.

The result is that harmful (as well as healthy) patterns of behaviour are inherited from the past. Families walk into the future backwards. At an unconscious level, they don't expect to change.

Don't want to change

Nor do they want to change. Frequently, these inherited rules are never challenged. Everyone in the family has a vested interest in the present arrangement and seeks to maintain it. This is one of the great paradoxes of family life. Outsiders can see how damaging the rules are, but insiders think it's the best deal they can get.

One of the insights of family therapy is that however unjust a domestic situation, everyone in it – even those who are suffering the greatest – believes they have most to gain by upholding the status quo. The family scapegoat who always gets the blame at least knows that he is not ignored. The daughter who feels 'got at' by her mother has the reward of seeing father come to her support. She feels reassured that despite his normal indifference, at least he will not abandon her.

The husband who feels unfairly henpecked by his wife is

---

2. Robin Skynner/John Cleese, *Families and How to Survive Them*, pp. 17–18.

compensated by having his childish needs met; his wife mothers the little boy inside him. He could change the situation if he was to 'grow up' and take more responsibility himself. But that would threaten his wife, who feels needed through her mothering role. It seems altogether safer to leave things as they are.

Paul, by contrast, faced a crisis at work. All his self-confidence evaporated. His bonhomie disappeared. Sylvia had never seen him so worried. For the first time in their marriage he began to lean on her. He looked to her for encouragement. He had dissipated so much nervous energy at work that he didn't have the strength to take the family decisions; he wanted Sylvia to do so. Instead of cracking all the jokes himself, he expected Sylvia to provide the sparkle at home.

It was more than Sylvia could bear. She had felt very comfortable being dependent on Paul. Decisions were taken out of her hands. She had no need to worry if things went wrong because they were Paul's responsibility. Coming so unexpectedly and quickly, the new situation made her feel totally insecure. Indeed, it made her so anxious that she became physically ill. And that solved the problem. Paul had to stay home to look after her. Once more he became the dominant partner and she the dependent wife. When he returned to the office, the crisis had passed.

Safety, the avoidance of anxiety, is a key pay-off to those who are damaged by families. Victims are rewarded for their suffering by not having to worry that things will get worse. This helps to explain why some of the most unjust family situations never come to light. The child who is sexually abused by her father may be frightened about what will happen to him if she is believed, and to her if she is not. So she remains silent.

Time and again therapists find that family members collude to keep things as they are. That is why family rules, however unfair and however much damage they inflict, have an enduring quality. Nobody wants to change.

Don't know how to change

I was among a group of students who were asked to recall a time when a family situation would have been helped by an outsider coming into it. There were forty of us on the course, and each of us remembered at least one occasion – the death of a sister, marital breakup, a conflict with parents – when outside help might have made a difference. We were squaring up to the failure of families to cope with crises on their own.

Dr Sheila Shinman, a researcher at London's Tavistock Institute, has shown how parents who most need help are deeply suspicious and even fearful of those who might provide it. They see potential helpers as a threat to their own weak sense of identity. 'I didn't like to let my health visitor know that I couldn't cope with my two children', said a doctor's wife. Some parents lack a sense of control over their lives. Fearful that fate is already out of their hands, all their instincts are to get back in charge. Seeking help runs in an opposite direction.[3]

A sociologist, Margaret O'Brien, has suggested why *men* do not seek help. Often they fail to recognise the need because they cope with family-induced stress by turning to alcohol or by becoming ill . Steve may think he has a back problem and go to his GP, rather than seeing it as a stress symptom caused by events at home. Men prefer to delegate family problems to their wives and don't see themselves as responsible for them. They are frequently reluctant to put their feelings into words, which is a key ingredient of therapy. They would rather be told what to do than to 'confess' their mistakes. Seeking advice is seen as a weakness. It is inconsistent with the self-reliance of the macho image.[4]

The result is that many families do not receive the help they need to change rules which treat their members unfairly. They are not helped to discuss what they are doing and how that affects individuals within the household. They are not encouraged to think about alternative models of behaviour. Their fears of change are not brought into the open by an outsider and allayed. They are not confronted with the need to do things differently by someone who can see the harm in what is going on. They are not shown practical steps to improve the situation. Many families are stuck with unfair rules of behaviour simply because they don't know how to change.

---

3. Dr Sheila Shinman, *A Chance for Every Child?* Tavistock 1981, pp. 78–9.
4. Margaret O'Brien, 'Men and Fathers in Therapy', *Journal of Family Therapy*, May 1988, pp. 45–51.

Don't have the energy to change

This is a fourth reason why unjust patterns of behaviour persist in families. Each of us has a picture in our minds of how we fit into the family. In the example earlier, Sylvia pictured herself as an obedient, devoted wife. Paul saw himself as the decision-maker. To change family behaviour, members have to redraw their mental pictures of the family. They have to sketch out in their minds what they are going to do differently at home.

Painting pictures requires energy, as Michelangelo must have realised as he wielded his brush on the roof of the Sistine Chapel. Redrawing mental pictures requires energy too. And many people do not have enough of it. They may be so busy coping with the stress of work that they lack the mental energy to change their view of family life. They may be so exhausted by looking after the family on their own that they have no emotional reserves left.

They may have felt so put down by their parents that they consume an unhealthy amount of energy asserting themselves. A disproportionate amount of energy may be devoted to burying the pain of losing a parent in childhood; hardly any is left to change how they see themselves at home. Anxiety about other people's reactions may syphon off energy that could have been used to redraw the family picture. Many people do not have enough energy to change their minds. Later we shall see how families can break the mould.

Psychology has been defined as the pursuit of the id by the odd. Yet the insights of psychologists who see the family as a system help us to understand why families can be so hurtful. Damaging rules of behaviour get handed down surreptitiously from one generation to another, so that families don't expect to change. Family members have a vested interest in the status quo, which means that they don't want to change. Because they are reluctant to seek help, they don't know how to change. Even if they did, often they would not have the energy to change.

Henry James tells a story about an artist who wanted to paint the perfect madonna. For twenty years he locked himself away and worked at the canvas. Finally, after he died, the painting was inspected and found to have been painted over and over so often that it was totally black. Many families hide themselves away and repeat over and over the same kind of behaviour. Their lives have become trapped in the dark.

3

Hurt by their morality

'The basic building block of society is shifting from the family to the individual', John Naisbitt declared in *Megatrends*, the book of trend projections that became a best seller in 1984, and the statistics seem to bear him out. In 1986 the US Census Bureau projected that, of the nineteen million households likely to be added to American society between 1987 and 2000, probably only three in ten will be husband-and-wife couples. The rest will be singles, single-parent families and couples cohabiting.[1]

Peter Berger and other sociologists are saying that this flight from the family is due to the radical individualism of the West. Modern people find meaning and a sense of who they are in their 'right to choose'. Fewer and fewer build their lives round their roles of mother, father, wife or husband. Their priority is to be fulfilled. 'I must be happy', 'I must express who I am', 'Don't condemn me to a life of limited fulfilment. Don't box me in with traditional morality. Let me be myself.'[2]

That is the cry of the liberal, 'self-please' ethic. It is *not* mere selfishness. All through the ages philosophers have recognised the selfish nature of men and women. But till quite recently they had noticed it by and large only to deplore it and urge its control by higher moral values. Even today, for example, practising Jews or Muslims will have a highly developed morality that tells them they have done wrong if they act selfishly.

What is new about the self-please morality is that it not only acknowledges human selfishness, but says that this is rational and morally defensible within limits. Selfishness is not morally wrong: it is morally right, so long as others are not hurt,

---

1. Quoted by Tim Keller, 'Anything do us part', *Eternity*, June 1987, pp. 20–3.
2. Peter and Brigitte Berger, *War over the Family*, pp. 111–2.

because each person has the right to realise their potential and seek fulfilment.

Indeed, selfishness is good for other people! So market forces should be encouraged, it is said, because as individuals pursue their (selfish) interests, buying what they want, other people will be encouraged to produce those goods, and this will create jobs, wealth and so on. Selfishness is good not just for the individual, but for the nation. 'If it seems to meet your needs and doesn't hurt anyone else,' the self-please morality says, 'follow the signpost marked "Pleasure ahead".'

This morality burst on the scene in the eighteenth century. Philosophers argued that individuals were not just members of society with obligations: they were autonomous individuals with rights – not least the right to freedom. These rights had to be protected, they said, which meant that the spotlight fell increasingly on the individual (and his or her rights) rather than the family or community. A few years later the Romantic Movement developed the idea of the personality. Individuals, it was argued, should develop their own personality to the greatest possible extent.

Put individual rights and personal development together, and you get the modern idea of the individual's right to personal fulfilment, or 'self-actualisation'. Psychologists like Alfred Maslow have helped to popularise this notion, so that the search for individual fulfilment is now perhaps *the* dominant feature of western culture.

In a way, this self-please morality reflects a Christian truth that God wants men and women to be fulfilled. He gave the first man and woman a beautifully designed garden so that they could enjoy it. It was 'pleasing to the eye and good for food' (Genesis 2:9). Jesus came into the world so that men and women might have fulness of life. The trouble is that it is an incomplete morality. It lacks the Christian insight into where true fulfilment can be found.

What are the effects of the self-please ethic on the family? A healthy family is one in which members are committed to each other, but where the commitment is not so intense that the other person feels stifled. Members care for one another, but also allow each other to breathe. There is a balance between relationships and personal autonomy. The self-please ethic wrecks that balance. Instead of commitment it encourages rejection, instead of respect for the other's autonomy it encourages emotional clinging. It does that in marriage and in parenting.

The effect on marriage

The demands on marriage have never been greater. Since 1851 average life expectancy in Britain has increased from 40 to 71 years for men and from 42 to 77 years for women. This casts an entirely new slant on the promise 'till death us do part'. Today's newly-weds, if they stay together, face half a century of marriage. During that time they will experience a degree of social, economic and personal change which is well-nigh unquantifiable.

At the same time, expectations of marriage have never been higher. It is expected to be more equal, with greater intimacy and sharing between partners, and to be more sexually fulfilling than ever before. Partners expect to be valued and appreciated, and to find meaning in their relationship. Newly-weds, by and large, expect their marriages to last.

Now if these expectations are to be met over half a century, partners have to learn how to be committed to each other without suffocating one another. The self-please morality encourages the opposite.

Rejection

In the June 1982 issue of *New Women*, which claims more than eight million readers, there was an extract from the book *Divorce: how and when to let go* by John and Nancy Adam.

> Yes, your marriage can wear out. People change their values and lifestyle. People want to experience new things. Change is part of life. Change and personal growth are traits for you to be proud of, indicative of a vital searching mind. You must accept the reality that in today's multi-faceted world it is especially easy for two persons to grow apart. Letting go of your marriage – if it is no longer good for you – can be the most successful thing you have ever done. Getting a divorce can be a positive, problem-solving, growth-oriented step. It can be a personal triumph.[3]

3. Quoted by John Stott, *Issues Facing Christians Today*. London 1984, p. 260.

So speaks the authentic voice of the self-please morality.

This attitude not only undermines commitment *within* marriage, it also undermines commitment *to* marriage. It has given rise to alternatives to legal marriage – to cohabitation where there is no permanent commitment at the outset, to open marriages where sexual commitment to one partner is abandoned, and to creative singleness where the person enters into sexual liaisons for shorter or longer periods without any expectation of commitment.

Lifelong commitment is seen as dangerous because it ties you down and stunts personal growth. People need the freedom to move in and out of deep relationships, it is said, so that they can become more fully themselves. Personal fulfilment is more important than surrender to someone else. So relationships are abandoned to the capriciousness of the personal, to the ebb and flow of hair-lines, waist-lines and bust-lines. The relationship is good for *me* so long as *I* still feel in love, so long as it is promoting *my* personal growth, so long as *I* am being fulfilled. If it stops meeting *my* needs, then I am entitled to start again.

One of the fiercest critics of this self-please approach is Robert H. Rimmer. Rimmer is best known for his advocacy of plural marriage in novels such as *The Harried Experiment* and *Proposition 31*. But he has attacked the 'unreal, impossible world of sexual freedom coupled with I-gotta-be-me interpersonal relationships. Most of them seem to be unaware that sexual hedonism as a way of life may be possible in the animal world but will not work for human beings.'

Rimmer believes that it is possible to be committed to deep love relationships with perhaps two or three people at a time. But he insists that the essence of a love relationship is not taking out of it what's in it for me (a pragmatic balancing of rewards and costs), but 'mental–sexual surrender' to the other person. In other words, it requires an ethic based on self-giving, not self-pleasing.[4]

Self-giving occurs when a wife is committed to her husband for life and says, 'Your interests are more important than mine', which is a massive affirmation of the husband's worth. This affirmation will help to undo the lack of appreciation the man may have felt as a boy. It occurs when a husband is committed

---

4. See Ross T. Bender, *Christians in Families: Genesis and Exodus*. Pennsylvania, Herald Press 1982, pp. 50–6.

in the same way to his wife, which is the most powerful demonstration of acceptance that a woman can have. It will help to undo the years of rejection she may have experienced as a child.

When a husband gives up some of the things he wanted to do (perhaps by staying home to look after the children), so that his wife can pursue her interests and develop her abilities, he helps to bring out the best in her. She may blossom in ways that were never encouraged before. When this self-giving is reciprocated over a lifetime, both partners will grow in security and realise more of their potential.

But this self-giving requires commitment. It requires the partners to resist the temptation to give up on each other when times get hard. It requires a willingness to persist even when they feel out of love. Often when partners do persist, when they go on giving to each other, they find that love returns.

Sometimes that doesn't happen, and with the best will in the world, separation still becomes inevitable. The trouble with the self-please ethic, however, is that it makes divorce more likely by undermining commitment. It creates a moral atmosphere in which the partners are more concerned about themselves than each other, and which encourages them to drift apart before giving the relationship a go. Fulfilment then becomes a lonely pursuit. It lacks the support of a partner who is prized and trusted. It becomes marred by the pain of rejection which undermines self-confidence and makes it more difficult to enter new relationships. The person may feel unfulfilled and become increasingly frustrated.

Clinging

Josh was very much into the self-please morality, though he would never have described it as such. Marriage for him was just another route to personal pleasure. He was intensely attracted to his wife, Debbie, and felt so good when he was close to her that he wanted her all the time.

But this possessiveness stifled her. It became an intrusive, manipulative force as he tried to control her, as he forced her to have sex when she would rather have gone to sleep, as he became jealous of her friends and afraid they would draw her away. Eventually she could stand it no longer, and left.

Josh was devastated. Those fears of rejection which he had

harboured since childhood, that sense that he was not really worth loving because his Dad never thought much of him, those fears exploded to the surface. So it was true. He actually wasn't worth loving. Not even his wife, who once thought the world of him, could put up with him any more. He ended up most evenings in the pub, in the hope that he would be valued by his friends and that the pain could be anaesthetised by drink.

The self-please ethic had put few boundaries around Josh's search for fulfilment through marriage. It had allowed him to violate Debbie's rights. He clung to her so tightly that she felt as if life was being squeezed out of her. The end result was that Josh's pursuit of fulfilment became the very thing that prevented him from finding the fulfilment he craved.

Parenting

Relationships between parents and children need that same balance as in marriage – between commitment to the other person and respect for their autonomy. Once again, the self-please ethic works in the opposite direction, toward rejection and clinging.

Rejection

Many parents are under so much pressure to pursue their own goals that they have little time for their children. Some of these pressures come from outside the family – the attractions of a blossoming career for example, or the need to find a job, whatever the hours, to avoid the isolation of home. Sometimes parents are so exhausted that they can do little more than flop in front of the television, scarcely even aware of the children, let alone caring for them. The children feel rejected. They see home as a place not of emotional warmth, but of indifference and emptiness.

Perhaps it is worth noting again that the self-please ethic reflects in a small way the Christian insight that God intends parents to be fulfilled. After all, if parents are fulfilled they will be better parents – they will be less tense, and it's more likely they will have wider interests which will give them more to share with their children. A balance is required between the needs of the parents and the needs of the child.

The ethic's emphasis on *self*-fulfilment, however, works against this balance. It allows parents to be more interested in their own fulfilment than their child's. It creates a moral atmosphere which encourages parents to give in to the attractions of work or their leisure pursuits, and to put these ahead of their children.

I remember my father, who was a doctor, telling me about a young woman who came to see him. She was distraught at how little her father cared for her. One evening, just to see what would happen, she pretended that she had become engaged. She burst into the front room where her father was watching television as he did every evening. 'Dad', she announced, 'I've just got engaged!' 'Oh,' came the reply, 'go and tell your mother about it.' The self-please morality creates an atmosphere which encourages parental self-indulgence, instead of checking it.

It also encourages parents to be over-tolerant. They may well adopt a 'child rights' approach, which says that a child has the right to choose for herself how to realise her potential, so long as she does not harm other people. But if a father's typical response is, 'Well, it's up to you. You decide', the teenager may wonder if her father's tolerance is not, in fact, a form of indifference. She may eventually feel rejected.

Clinging

Children may suffer from clinging as well as rejection. Many parents are highly manipulative. They invade their children's autonomy and force them to do what they want. Sometimes they cling to the child so tightly that her personality is destroyed.

This can occur if parents are controlled by the psychological drives which lie frequently behind the decision to parent. Many parents have children so that they can feel they have arrived as adults; so that they can feel loved, wanted and needed; so that they can outshine other couples by having better children or by being more successful parents; or so that the children can succeed in areas where they failed.

Children often become pawns in parental attempts to meet these needs. The son is expected to do the sports in which his father had wanted to excel. The daughter is pushed to keep up with the girl down the road. But if the boy turns more readily to books than to football, Dad loses interest. Mother will secretly blame her daughter if she is not good enough. The tiny baby who cries instead of snuggling up to her mum senses the resentment of a woman who desperately needs to be loved.

Each of these children is made – unfairly – to feel a failure, because they cannot meet the needs which drove Mum and Dad to have them in the first place. Instead of being respected as individuals with their own needs, they are expected to meet the needs of their parents. The parents live through their children. They cling to them by imposing their ambitions on them, and the children feel crushed.

The self-please ethic provides a rationalisation for this. The mother who decides to have children because she wants to be fulfilled through parenting, or because she has the right to have children, is justifying her decision in terms of the self-please morality. She is giving a moral pretext for children, when the real reason may be more deep-seated.

The result is that her underlying motives are given a moral disguise. The disguise fits comfortably because it is similar to the underlying reasons for parenting. Like them, it says that Mum's needs should be met through children. But the real motives lurk, unchecked, ready to influence how the children are brought up. They encourage the mother to impose her ambitions on the child. And the self-please morality will do little to stop her, because it comes too close to these motives to check them: it is focused on the self, just as the underlying motives are focused on the self.

Christians would say that though God wants parenting to be fulfilling, part of the key to that is not to pursue self-fulfilment but the fulfilment of the child. This produces a morality with a strong orientation away from the self, and which provides a counterweight to the selfish drives which often lie behind the decision to parent.

So a mother who has a baby because of a need to feel loved, will be less likely to see her child as a means to her own acceptance and become angry with him when he fails to show her the love she craves. She will feel under a moral obligation to do the best for her child. Instead of a morality which makes it easier for her to give in to her selfish needs, she will be driven by a morality which encourages her to rise above those needs.

What is wrong with the self-please morality?

Why is it that the self-please morality encourages rejection and clinging in families? There are at least three reasons. First, it is a morality which emphasises the person more than the relationship. It is a *self*-please morality. It is individuals who count. Ultimately they owe no allegiance to any authority but themselves. They are autonomous. So they are not bound by the authority of any relationship. The demands of a relationship are secondary to their rights as people.

Yet the essence of family is not individuals, but the relationships between them – between husband and wife, between parents and children, between the children, between the nuclear family and other relatives. Hurt is caused when an individual rides roughshod over these relationships – when the man piles up complaints against his wife, when the mother gives up on the child, or when the daughter acts up to force her parents to do what she wants.

By emphasising the person, the self-please morality makes it harder for the individual to resist putting his own interests before other people's. It makes it less likely that he will seek a balance of interests, which is what fair relationships are all about. Bedan Mbugua heads up the Family Development Trust in Kenya's capital city, Nairobi. He recalls:

> I lost my parents when I was very young, so I grew up with lots of support from other family members. I could stay with any member of the family whenever I wanted to, so I had no feelings of loneliness. . . In most of Africa the whole family (including uncles, grandparents and so on) still contributes to raising the money to send children to school. . . When families are strong they can support individuals through very hard times. In Uganda, many people have only been able to withstand the troubles because they are able to rely so strongly on the family. It provides a strong network of people.

By contrast, Bedan went on,

> the whole of western thought is geared towards independence from the family. School training is aimed at preparing children to achieve economic self-reliance. . . But self-reliance and independence are in the end an illusion. People always

need to be loved and cared for. They can never exist on their own. People cannot ultimately be satisfied with independence. The western ideology of independence can mean denying oneself the best source of love and care.[5]

By encouraging self-reliance and independence the self-please ethic comes too close to selfishness to prevent selfishness.

Secondly, the self-please morality emphasises pleasure more than sacrifice. Self-fulfilment typically involves the pursuit of what makes the individual feel good. It is the pursuit of gratification, of pleasure. This runs totally against the pursuit of justice, which frequently requires the sacrifice of pleasure in the interests of someone else. Responsible parents make sacrifices for their children, compassionate children do the same for their ageing parents, husbands and wives give up things for each other.

When they don't, damage is done. The child grows up bitterly resentful because he was unfairly neglected, the elderly are left – alone – on the edge of society, the marriage partner is ill-treated by their spouse. An ethic which makes pleasure a goal is in no position to prevent others being hurt. It is too far from self-sacrifice to promote self-sacrifice.

Thirdly, the self-please morality emphasises the present more than the future. The search for self-fulfilment encourages a 'living for now' attitude. How can you know whether the search has been successful? Only by whether you feel fulfilled. When do you have those feelings? In the present. The here-and-now becomes all important.

But caring at home often requires that the future should have priority. The mother who gives up a rewarding job for a while to look after her baby and is kept awake for most of the night, may have very little sense of fulfilment. But she will be treating her child kindly by investing in its future. The husband who declines a job in another city because his wife needs to stay where they are, is investing in the future of his marriage. The self-please ethic, by contrast, is too caught up with the present to care about the future.

It is a morality which puts so much stress on the person, on pleasure and on the present that it is unable to keep a balance between commitment to the other person and that person's

5. *Familybase News*, 2, 1987.

independence. It creates a moral atmosphere which encourages either rejection or intrusion.

Karen Blixen, feminist writer and author of *Out of Africa* (later to become the award-winning film), wrote in an essay on marriage: 'It is sadly true that if most of the older people alive today were to look back over their lives, they would have to acknowledge that their most contemptible behaviour as human beings had been in connection with love.'[6] In chapters 1 and 2 we looked at the social and psychological pressures on families. In this chapter we have seen how the self-please ethic is too close to selfishness to prevent selfishness. All too often it allows family love to become contemptible.

---

6. Karen Blixen, *On Modern Marriage and Other Observations*, p. 57.

PART TWO
Envisioned families

4

Spreading out

Recently I asked parents in a shopping precinct why they had had children. One or two said that their children were accidents. The rest were slightly bemused. The question had never occurred to them. Having children was natural, 'something you just do'. But as people thought about it, they replied in much the same way: 'Because we like children', 'Because we thought it would be fun', 'Because we wanted them'. Having children, it seems (and larger surveys bear this out), is something parents do to be more fulfilled.

This reflects, perhaps, the joy God wants parents to have through parenting. Presumably it also reflects in part a deep instinct to perpetuate the human race. Scripture acknowledges that instinct by suggesting that families create God's family. The goal of individual families is to create a world-wide family which reflects the character of God. Commitment to that goal will increase the joy of parenting and help the family find fulfilment.

In the case of those shoppers who replied, 'because we wanted children', behind their desire to be parents may have been a scarcely acknowledged hope that their child would make them feel that they had arrived as adults, or that he would make them feel important because they were responsible for another person's life, or perhaps that he would succeed where Dad had failed, or that he would give Mum a role in life, or that he would hold together a crumbling marriage.

All these are common enough reasons for having children, as we saw in the last chapter, but they are not enough to sustain commitment. What happens when the sense of being an adult no longer depends on having a child, or if Mum and Dad come to feel totally inadequate as parents, or if the child is handicapped, or Mum gets bored with her new role, or if the marriage falls apart?

When parenting becomes tough and the initial reasons for having children disappear, when Mum is exhausted by three children and Dad is exhausted by work, parents need a vision beyond the child to keep them committed to their task. That is one reason why Scripture's vision of building God's family is so important.

The approach

But why turn to the Bible? Why not rely on the insights of the caring professions and the social sciences to address the issues in part 1? Isn't it sufficient to study how families function healthily in the real world rather than turn to a book which is thousands of years old?

The answer depends on how we think God communicates with men and women. Christians have long believed that God does speak through our observation of the world – that we can learn, for example, something of God's desire for family life by looking at how healthy families behave in practice. But Christians have also traditionally believed that God speaks in a special way through the experiences and insights of the human authors of Scripture, and that God's will – which is sometimes only dimly revealed in 'nature' – is often more fully revealed in the Bible.

We shall want to pay particular attention, therefore, to what God says through Scripture. That is not to say that the Bible should be read in isolation from our observations of how the world best works: rather, it should be read in relation to the world, in a dialogue together, so that both can throw light on each other.

Of course we have to be very careful about how we apply Scripture to family situations today. The cultural gap between when it was written and the modern world is immense. And so we need to distinguish between what was addressed to a particular culture (such as Paul requiring women to cover their heads), and underlying principles which are valid for all time.

One way of doing this is to look for themes which are common to the Old and New Testaments. This is because the Bible itself contains literature which originates in different cultures. Themes which span these cultures by running from the beginning of Scripture to the end are more likely to apply to all people, whatever their culture, than instructions which are addressed to one particular situation within Scripture.

In the next few chapters we shall look first at the Old and then at the New Testaments. We shall see how in the Old Testament Israelite families were expected to create a global family where knowledge of God was passed from one generation to the next, and in which relationships were characterised by freedom, equality and solidarity. We shall then see how these themes are repeated, but with an additional twist, in the New Testament. Finally, we shall see how they provide a very positive approach to the issues in part 1.

The first family

The American President, Lyndon Johnson, once said, 'We live in a world that has narrowed into a neighbourhood before it has broadened into a brotherhood.' The Bible's vision for the family is wider than the home and the neighbourhood: it is global in scope. The family is to help create a world-wide community whose members feel part of a single mega-family.

This vision is hinted at in Genesis 1 – 2. God fathers the first man and woman. He creates them. He cares for them – by planting a garden for them. He passes on to them a set of moral values, summed up in the command not to eat from the tree of knowledge of good and evil. He gives them responsibility – to rule over the earth – just as good parents increase a child's responsibilities as he or she matures. Adam and Eve were children of God.

They in turn were given children not so that they could simply enjoy the delights of parenting. If Adam and Eve had been asked, 'Why did you have children?', their answer would have been very different to the replies of those Monday-morning shoppers. Adam and Eve had children so that their family might one day spread over the whole world. 'God blessed them and said to them, "Be fruitful and increase in number; fill the earth and subdue it" ' (Gen. 1:28). Among other creation narratives of the ancient Near East, this emphasis on one great family is unique to Genesis. The Old Testament scholar, Th. C. Vriezen, notes that the other creation narratives describe the formation of certain towns or nations. By contrast, Adam and Eve were to give birth to a united global family.[1]

A new family

Genesis goes on to describe how the first man and woman failed to create that family. Family relationships became contaminated by sin. At Babel their family fragmented. Adam and Eve's descendants broke into factions and scattered as separate families over the earth (Gen. 11:1ff). The global family disintegrated.

Yet in spite of the Fall, the family as a social institution retains its goodness. Though relationships *within* the family have been marred by sin, the task given to the family at creation remains. Much of Scripture (though it is concerned also with institutions other than the family) can be read as an attempt to limit the effects of sin on family relationships, so that the family can achieve God's original purpose for it. Families are to help roll back evil in the world, despite being damaged by the Fall.

So Genesis describes how God establishes the nation of Israel to reverse Babel's fragmentation of humanity. She was to become a planet-wide family by growing in size and absorbing the surrounding peoples. Individual families were to build this wider family.

Children were given to Abraham explicitly for this purpose. No mention is made of sparing Sarah the acute social disgrace at the time of being infertile, nor of giving her a chance to express her maternal instincts. These considerations were less important than God's ultimate goal. The Lord said to Abraham, 'I will make you into a great nation and I will bless you . . . all peoples on earth will be blessed through you' (Gen. 12:2–3).

Each family descended from Abraham was to continue the task of creating this wider family. One way was by bringing foreigners into the nation. Non-Israelite women taken in battle could join the community through marriage (Deut. 21:10ff). Residence in an Israelite home brought foreign slaves into the

---

1. Th. C. Vriezen, *An Outline of Old Testament Theology*. Blackwell, Oxford 1962, p. 216.

community (Gen. 17:12f). But the most important way was by having children.

That was one reason why procreation was so important. When the cellist Jacqueline du Pré died the newscaster remarked that her memory lives on. It was even more important to Israelites that their memory, too, should go on. It meant that their life had been significant. People would remember what they had done. To die and not be remembered would speak volumes about how meaningless their life had been.

A man's memory lived on by the continuation of his 'name'. For in Israelite society a name was more than a name. It told you something about the person's character, just as the surname 'Smith' used to indicate a man's job. If an Israelite's name survived his death, it meant that a person's character continued to live on in the community.

This happened through the family. The man passed on part of his character to his children – genetically (in modern parlance) and in the way he brought them up. The children in turn passed on something of that same character to their children. So after even a number of generations a man's character was still important. It was the shoot that had become part of the family tree. As the tree grew in size, with more and more branches, so would the nation.

As one of the building blocks of an individual family, therefore, the character (or 'name') of a person helped to create the national community. A man would die, but who he was and what he had done would have lasting results. Survival of the family guaranteed the survival of his contribution – through his descendants – to a community which was no ordinary community, but one with a global role.

No wonder Israelites were fascinated by genealogies! Genealogies reminded them that individuals who were often historically unimportant had played a vital part in building the people of God.

The Israelites had a custom, known as the levirate, which ensured that if a man died childless his 'name' would be perpetuated. His widow was to marry her husband's brother and they were to have children 'for' the dead man (Deut. 25:5–10). Some years ago the Old Testament scholar, Johs Pederson, explained the significance:

If a man, after having contracted marriage, dies without sons, then he dies entirely. It is this blotting out of life which is to be avoided. His nearest of kin, the brother, must perform this office of love in order to protect him from extermination. The wife, whose object in life is to bear him a son in whom his life is resurrected, must be enabled to do her duty towards him.[2]

Though the dead man had died, his character would not die entirely with him. The dead man's life would be reborn in his nephew at least to some extent, because his brother would share some of his characteristics and pass them on to the new son. At a genetic level a nephew must have something in common with his uncle.

This deep-seated desire for the family to make a permanent contribution to God's people gave life a strong sense of purpose. Though a person physically died, his life continued to have meaning. What he did in the family now, how he treated his wife or how he behaved toward his children, would be significant years later because it would be yet another influence on what the family was to become. His family would help to create the nation of God.

Families would also help the nation to grow when their elders took part in the local administration of justice (so promoting social stability), when they provided recruits for the army (enabling the nation to defend itself) and when they added to the nation's wealth by producing crops and other goods for people to buy. Stability, security and prosperity would increase the nation's power, enabling it to extend its borders and to attract foreigners to settle within them.

Israel was to grow *through* families. She was also to grow *into* a family. We have seen that an important feature of family life is the closeness of its members. What one person does has a strong impact on the others. Mum's behaviour has a tremendous influence on Dad and on the baby. There is probably no other social group in which the behaviour of one person has such a profound effect on the others. The nation of Israel seems to have had a similar sense of family closeness. When David was anointed king, the whole of Israel said, 'We are your own flesh and blood' (2 Sam. 5:1).

The people thought of themselves as one family. In contrast to Babylon which took its name from a city, the Israelites

2. Johs Pederson, *Israel: Its Life and Culture*, p. 78.

described themselves by a family name – Israel. Their division into tribes named after Israel's sons reflected a sense of belonging to Israel's family.

Each generation felt acutely that it belonged to the same family as its ancestors and descendants. That is why God could address the contemporaries of Amos as 'the whole family which I brought up out of the land of Egypt', even though that event had happened hundreds of years before (Amos 3:1).

It is significant that the Hebrew word for 'house', *beth*, which referred to the smallest family unit, was also used of the entire nation (the 'house of Israel'). Likewise the word for people, *am*, which was used of the nation, originally referred to close relatives. Even if they did not know each other, Israelites still regarded themselves as 'brothers' (e.g. Exod. 2:11; Lev. 10:6; Deut. 15:3; Jer. 34:14). How naturally will a New Yorker describe a Californian as 'brother', or a Londoner be called 'brother' by a stranger from Liverpool?

As 'brothers', the Israelites knew that one person's actions could affect the national family as a whole. So when Achan disobeyed God and looted Jericho, the whole nation was expected to feel involved (Josh. 7:1, 11). If this seems strange, it is not so far removed from the shame many in England felt after English soccer fans rioted in the Heysel stadium in Belgium during 1985.

A lot of people felt that the violence somehow reflected on them because they were part of the same nation. The Israelites had a similar sense of being involved in each other's sin; but their family-like closeness meant that they felt it more intensely, just as a mother may feel disgraced by her child.

Individual families, then, were to build not only a people, but a family. This family was to become like God by keeping God's laws, for these laws expressed God's character (just as the laws of a democracy will express a country's political character). Surrounding nations were to see what God was like because he was to be mirrored in the people's life (Exod. 19:6).

'Like father, like son.' God was to be Israel's Father and Israel his Son (e.g. Exod. 4:22; Deut. 32:6; Isa. 63:16; Hos. 11:1). As foreigners were attracted to this God-like family and converted to Judaism, the nation was to increase in size (Psalm 87). It would become 'a light for the Gentiles, that it might bring God's salvation to the ends of the earth' (Isa. 49:6). Each family was to help build this global family.

A home for the family

Individual families were also to create a physical environment fit for this world family. That is clear from Genesis 1 – 2, where the command to master the environment is given to the man and the woman together (Gen. 1:27f). As the family grew they were to push back the boundaries of the Garden of Eden, till eventually the whole world had become a domestic garden for their descendants.

Now it might be argued that this command is given to men and women in general rather than to families in particular. For Genesis 1 – 3 contain principles that are meant to apply not only to marriage, but to human relationships as a whole. However, in Genesis 1:28 there is a significant link between procreation (which was to be done in a family context) and mastering the world. There is also a link in Genesis 2 between work and the man's need for a marital, 'one flesh' companion to help him in it. Mastering the world was to be a *family* task.

'Subduing' the world (1:28) involves mastering the laws of nature. How else can it be done? Humankind was to master musical, sporting, scientific and countless other natural laws to create a magnificent culture in which to house God's family. Each generation was to make its contribution, as layer upon layer was added to civilisation. The glories of modern and past civilisations hint at how stupendous the result might have been if men and women had stayed loyal to God.

This task remained with families after the Fall. In the Canaanite city states around Israel all land was owned by the king, and those who lived and worked on it owed certain obligations to him. By contrast, land in Israel was parcelled into family holdings, and various laws existed to prevent land passing out of the family's hands (e.g. Lev. 25:8ff).

It was assumed that family members would cultivate the land together. They were to do this in ways that reduced the conflict between humanity and nature introduced by the Fall. Animal life was to be protected (Lev. 25:7). The soil was to be rested every seven years, which would have preserved its fertility (Lev. 25:1ff). The environment (which was an issue long before Europe's Green Parties took it up!) was not to be ravaged, but protected for successive generations. The future welfare of God's family would thus be secured (Lev. 25:18ff; cf. Deut. 22:6f).

It was through the land that the family was to be blessed, and these blessings were to take the form of agricultural fruitfulness (Deut. 28:1ff). Presumably it was on the back of this prosperity that Israel was to build a civilisation. So it was that through a combination of their own efforts and divine blessing, families were to create an environment fit for the family of God.

A vision for work and home

Families were to be committed to a vision – to a vision outside the nuclear family. They were not to turn in on themselves. They were to look outwards as they helped to create a global family and a home for that family. That at least was the intention: later we shall see how families failed to achieve fully what God planned for them, and how despite their failure God in his love found a way for families still to contribute to his purpose.

Assuming it is echoed in the New Testament, why is this vision important for homes today? The answer is that it gives a place to single people, a purpose to families and a perspective to work and home. It gives a place to single people because family is seen in broad, inclusive terms.

Modern society tends to put tight boundaries around the family. 'The family' is the nuclear family plus a few relatives. Others are outside the family. Single people in their late twenties or older often feel excluded. 'One frequently hears glowing accounts of "our church family" ', one single person wrote, 'but then is shattered to realise that this only provides for the nuclear family.'

The Old Testament blurs the distinction between the nuclear family and those outside it. The smallest family unit was to build a national family, which was to become a global family. Brotherhood was to extend way beyond the home. In Israel the whole community was the household of faith, including 'the stranger within your gates'. Families were to help build a community in which everyone felt at home.

They can start doing that today when, for example, they combine to form local communities – small churches are just one possibility – in which single and homeless people are made to feel 'part of the family', where outsiders are welcomed in and where bridges are built to those on the fringe of society.

Secondly, the vision gives a purpose to families. It provides a strong counter to the self-please ethic which can be so damaging to families. We saw in the last chapter how the self-please ethic creates a moral atmosphere which undermines commitment to relationships. It encourages the individual to do what he or she wants, so that family ties are neglected.

However, by setting a clear goal for the family, the Old Testament encourages family members to draw together in mutual support. Just as team members back each other up to win the game, so individuals will give to others in the family as they pursue their common goal. So when pressures mount and love grows cold, when spouses are tempted to be unfaithful, when parents become so busy with their friends that they ignore their children, recalling their family's task in the world can encourage husband and wife to renew their commitment to one another and to their children.

Thirdly, the vision gives a perspective to work and home, though we need to be tentative about this until we have looked at the New Testament, to check if Genesis simply reflects a primitive culture. Yet may it not, possibly, be significant that before the Fall work is set in the context of family, and that the task of building God's family was given to families? There was to be none of that conflict between work and home which has left 'families on the edge' of modern society.

This perhaps provides a check against being over absorbed in work. It reminds us that if work comes before home we neglect something that is important to God. God wants families to build up his family. They can do that by playing an active part in the church and by their involvement in the neighbourhood. They can become a bridge between the community of non-belief and the community of faith. The family has been given a mission, and the person who is totally wrapped up in his or her job underestimates the importance of that mission.

A little girl asked her mother, 'Why does Daddy bring so much work home at night?' 'Because he can't get it all done in the office,' Mother explained. 'Then why doesn't he join a slower group?' came the reply.

5

Passing on

Steve and Jean had just been thrown out of her parent's home. Her parents had never approved of Steve. Things had finally come to a head when Jean's mum had tried to hit Steve and Jean had intervened. . . Now Jean was looking for a bed. Her parents had always been dogmatic, she complained, they had thrust religion down her throat and their rigid discipline had been backed by sporadic outbursts of violence. 'I just can't take it any more!'

Later the parents described how they had wanted to bring up children who would share their Christian faith. But despite their good intentions, in practice their discipline had become an instrument of power. It had become a means of forcing the children to do what the parents wanted. Violence was triggered by fear that their power – and their 'success' as parents – was slipping away.

Violence was part of Peter's family too. His mother, Kate, was terrified of failing her children and turning them against her. She avoided confrontation because she dreaded those words and looks which would make her feel rejected. The family was chaotic. The three children were perpetually at war. Father was hardly ever there. Kate would first scream at the children, and then plead with them, but to no avail. Eventually their father would explode in a violent attempt to regain the control he'd never had. Peter could stand it no more. He inflicted bruises on himself so that he would be taken into care.

In Jean's family violence reinforced rigid discipline, in Peter's it was a pathetic substitute for discipline. There are plenty of families like them, and many others where parental power is more subtly abused or abdicated. The Old Testament shows how children should be brought up – justly.

In this chapter we shall look at parenting and then at children's response to their parents. The next chapter will focus on marriage. Dealing with the parent–child relationship before marriage contrasts with some books which start with marriage and then go on to parenting, and in so doing perhaps make it seem that marriage is at the heart of family. Single people are left feeling that they are outside family because they are unmarried. One of the themes of this book is that the parent-child relationship is pivotal to family life, and that makes the concept of family more inclusive of those who are single.

Gaining a friend

Love, teaching and discipline

Perhaps inevitably the Israelites shared many assumptions of the surrounding cultures, in which fathers had far greater authority than in modern society. Almost total obedience was expected of children. If a son disobeyed his father, it could bring social disgrace on the family. Villagers would want to know what was wrong with the man, and by implication the rest of the family, that his authority carried so little weight.

The Old Testament does not challenge these assumptions directly. Rather, it can be seen as containing principles which, depending on the degree to which they were implemented, might have undermined the prevailing culture from within. Families were to recognise the accepted legal position of fathers, but paternal authority itself was to have been exercised in a more 'enlightened' way. Slowly the nation was to pull away from the norms of the people round about, till eventually laws like the stoning of persistently disobedient children (Deut. 21:18ff), which was imported from the surrounding culture, would have been changed too. Old Testament morality started where the people were so that it could lead them to a higher ideal.

So, having accepted the father's near-total authority, it then 'humanised' that authority by assuming it would be accompanied by love. God is revealed as the nation's Father who cares for the people and guards them as the apple of his eye, and who is moved by love for his 'child' (Exod. 4:22; Deut. 32:6, 10; Hos. 11:1ff). 'As a father has compassion on his children,' Psalm 103:13 says, 'so the Lord has compassion on those that fear him.' The Israelites would have had difficulty singing and understanding that if they had not come to share the assumption that fathers loved their children.

It is clear that King David had strong feelings of love for his son Absalom, though these feelings got the better of him and were not matched by adequate discipline (2 Sam. 13:39; 18:33). Proverbs 13:24 puts discipline firmly in the context of love – it is out of love that the father disciplines his child. Deuteronomy 6:7 puts teaching into a similar context because it takes for granted that parents spend time with their children and that their communication is good. Love requires communication.

It was in this framework of love that parents were to teach children God's laws. This was not to be law in the sense of legalism, which often lies behind the attitude, 'Children ought to be brought up better these days'. At the heart of the Old Testament is law in the sense of Torah, 'the way things are'. Parents were to teach children the way things are.

They were to unfold God's harmony into which men and women were made to fit, and which they ignore to their cost and to the cost of the community. *Shalom*, well-being, would come if the children chose Torah. Knowing God's law would also enable the children to discover what God was like, for God's character was reflected in his laws (just as a mother's character is reflected in the rules she lays down for her children).

Parents were to teach God's laws with conviction. 'These commandments that I give you today are to be upon your hearts' (Deut. 6:6). They were to communicate a living faith which permeated every sphere of life (Deut. 6:7f; Prov. 6:20ff). They were to avoid, therefore, passing on an empty-shell religion which a child would see through and despise.

The little girl in *Punch* who had justified her use of a certain unmaidenly expression by the plea that 'Daddy says it', only to be told that 'Daddy is Daddy', is reported to have replied, 'Well, I'm I'm'.[1] By contrast, Old Testament parents were to explain their faith so that it did not appear irrational and unconvincing.

Explanations were to be given sensitively – in response to questions (Deut. 6:20ff); they were to be given when the child was ready to learn. The son was not to be swamped by ideas he could not grasp, nor were reasons to be withheld when the

1. Quoted by John Baillie, *Invitation to Pilgrimage*. OUP, 1942, p. 37.

daughter wanted to know. Appropriate knowledge was to be given at the right stage of the child's development. It was more likely that it would then be taken to heart.

Parents were to back their teaching with discipline. Proverbs goes so far as to say, 'he who spares the rod hates his son' (Prov. 13:24). This seems strangely unfashionable to many people. But 'rod' implies more than physical force. It can also be translated 'sceptre', which is a symbol of authority (Gen. 49:10; Ps. 45:6). Proverbs may be talking about the proper exercise of authority rather than just physical punishment.

A rod was also used by shepherds to guide and protect. It was a source of comfort to the sheep. So David could say, 'Your rod and your staff, they comfort me' (Ps. 23:4). Discipline was to be of comfort to a child. It was to show that parents were involved with him; the child's behaviour was important enough to be worth worrying about. And if his behaviour mattered, that meant the child mattered – which is why discipline builds a child's self-esteem.

The goal of parenting

Genesis 18 describes one of God's dramatic appearances to Abraham. Abraham is resting in the middle of the day, and looks up to find three men standing nearby. In some way these men represent the Lord. Abraham brings them food, they converse and then the men prepare to leave.

As Abraham walks with them to bid them farewell, the Lord says,

> Shall I hide from Abraham what I am about to do? Abraham will surely become a great and powerful nation, and all nations on earth will be blessed through him. For I have chosen him, so that he will direct his children and his household after him to keep the way of the Lord by doing what is right and just. . . (18:17ff)

God reveals that Abraham has been chosen to pass on to his children and their children how to obey God, 'how to keep the way of the Lord'. He is to teach his children what is right and just, and they are to pass this knowledge on to their children, so that Abraham's 'household after him' will know how to follow God.

The Lord therefore decides to tell Abraham about his plan

to destroy Sodom and Gomorrah. Abraham was to relay this to his children, so that his descendants could have before them an example of God's punishment of the wicked, and – as it turns out – of his willingness to spare the innocent. The example would be a lesson to Abraham's 'household': if they followed God they would be spared because they were innocent, if they did not they would be punished like the inhabitants of the two cities. Abraham's task as a parent, then, was to pass on to his children knowledge of the Lord, so that his entire family – which was meant to become a global family – would remain loyal to God.

Deuteronomy 6 makes the same point. Parenting was for more than the family: it was to strengthen the community. Instructions on how to parent were given to the whole people ('Hear, O Israel', vv. 3, 4) so that they might fear the Lord, have a long life and enjoy good fortune in the land (vv. 2f, 24f). Good parenting was to keep the *nation* – God's family – loyal to the Lord, and bring it stability and prosperity.

This stress on the community may seem strange because our society tends to see parenting in terms of the individual. Where parents have goals at all they tend to be of the kind, 'I did it for her own good', 'I only wanted his happiness'. Yet even so, parents normally hope that their children will contribute to society in some way. If their children fail to do so, if they fail grossly by being convicted of a crime for example, parents will usually feel acutely embarrassed. This is partly because the parents think the failure is their failure. But it is often also because they will sense that the whole community has suffered.

Parents who want their children to be happy tend to believe that happiness will come from being a success in society. Contributing to society is a means to an end, the child's happiness. The Old Testament heightens this community dimension so that it becomes an end in itself, and defines success as the creation of a godly community. Parents could feel that they had arrived when their child threw himself into that community. Instead of being concerned merely for the child's happiness, parents were to be good parents for the sake of society.

Modern research suggests that the Old Testament's principles of love, teaching and discipline were – in all likelihood – well suited to achieving their goal. One study of 2600 teenagers found that children who feel strongly supported (i.e. loved) by their parents will tend to accept parental values; they will be even more likely to do so if the parents exercised discipline. When children feel unsupported, they will be more likely to choose different values.[2]

Later we shall see how the sinfulness of Israelite families meant that these principles were often ignored. But we shall also see that thanks to the cross, despite the fallen nature of the family, modern parents can still help to build God's family by loving, teaching and disciplining their children.

Being encouraged

Most parents know that they ought to love, teach and discipline their children. What they find difficult is keeping a balance between the three. One reason for this is because they are anxious – they worry that they won't succeed in giving their child the best. And so they over-compensate. If they are afraid of being too strict on the child, as Kate was, they react by becoming too lenient. If they are worried that they will show too much love (without enough discipline), as with Jean's parents, they react by becoming excessively strict.

The Old Testament's stress on the goal of parenting can help to reassure parents. It reminds them that just as an electric plug requires three pins, parenting needs each of its prongs of love, teaching and discipline. All three had to be involved if Israelite parents were to pass on the faith to their children. Indeed, since families were to have a key role in creating God's family, to a large extent the very success of God's plan for the world depended upon the three prongs existing together. Keeping these strands in balance was the most effective way that parents could persuade children to share their faith.

There is a promise therefore. Parents who seek this balance have every chance of passing their values on to their children and so winning their children. Because one of the biggest compliments a child can pay to his parents is to choose their values for himself. It means that he admires his parents, and unlike the rebel who despises his mother and father, admiration keeps a child loyal. Shared values also produce friendships, for friends never declare, 'we have nothing in common'.

Parents, then, who want to gain a friend will approach their task with this balance in mind. If they shrink from discipline

2. Ray S. Anderson and Dennis B. Guernsey, *On Being Family: A Social Theology of the Family*. Eerdmans, Grand Rapids 1985, pp. 132–6.

because they fear damaging their child or being rejected by her, they will be reassured to know that discipline is designed to win their daughter. She is more likely to be hurt and to reject her parents if she is not disciplined.

Parents who are afraid of spoiling their son and being too lenient may be encouraged to remember that love is one of the prongs as well. That will help them not to become too overbearing and harsh. Remembering the goal of parenting can be an encouragement. We can lean on whichever part of the triad – love, teaching or discipline – frightens us most. Because we know it was put there so that parents could create God's family by winning the respect of their children.

Letting go

Mao Ts-tung had a slogan, 'When the best leader's work is done, the people say "We did it ourselves" '. That would have been an apt motto for Israelite parents, for the Old Testament contains strong hints that children were to *choose* their religious beliefs so that they could say, 'we found it ourselves'.

Israelite parents were not to raise a child who was so indoctrinated that he reached 'copy-cat' conclusions the same as theirs. Nor were they to teach him to choose what *he* wanted, which is a modern view. They were to raise children with the ability to choose what *God* wanted, and to do that the child had to be given a choice. Parents were to provide that choice by teaching children the law. The children could then decide if it was worth keeping. Not to have taught the law would have taken that choice away.

At the same time, children were to be spiritually weaned so that they could own the faith for themselves and say, 'I believe this not just because my parents taught it to me, but because I myself have discovered it to be true.' They were to make a deliberate *decision* for God.

So Deuteronomy's reference (Deut. 6:20) to children asking parents the meaning of the law assumes that parents will raise inquiring children, and questioning children make up their own minds. The trouble is that they don't always accept the answers they are given! The Old Testament is realistic enough to know that whatever the parents do, children may become rebels and despise, mock or curse their parents (Prov. 15:20; 20:20; 30:11, 17).

Popular psychology has stressed the influence of parents on children to such an extent that if anything goes wrong parents immediately think it must be their fault. That was one reason why Jean's parents tried too hard, and with disastrous results, to bring her up as a Christian.

It is significant, then, that Israelite parents were not held accountable for the sins of their adult offspring. Deuteronomy 24:16 says that 'Fathers shall not be put to death for their children, nor children put to death for their fathers; each is to die for his own sins' (cf. Ezek. 18:1ff). Having done their best, parents had no need to blame themselves if a child rejected their spiritual values. They could teach without getting taut.

For a child to own her parents' faith, she had to become emotionally independent of them. The faith would then be her's and not her parents'. The need to separate from parents is brought out in Genesis 2:24, 'a man will leave his father and mother and be united to his wife'.

When Israelite couples got married, the woman would normally leave her family and move in with the man. This was symbolised during the wedding ceremony when the bride was brought across the village from her home to her husband's. Perhaps that is why there is no reference in this verse to the woman leaving home. Everyone knew that she would. And presumably a physical break led to an emotional one.

The stress on the man leaving his parents is highly significant. New couples would not always set up home immediately. They might live with the husband's parents for a while. When they did move into their own house, usually it would be only a short walk away. The son would stay near his father to help work the family farm. Genesis 2:24, therefore, implies not that the man was to leave his parents geographically: he was to leave them emotionally. He would then be free to reach his *own* decisions.

Mark Twain quipped, 'When I was 17 I thought my father was a fool. When I was 24 I was surprised how much he had learnt in such a short time.' Israelite parents were to raise children who, having come to their own conclusions, were surprised that their parents had got there first!

Respecting your parents

Why it was important in Israel

It was vital that the child should respect his parents if he was to adopt their faith and make it his own. That is one reason why the Old Testament emphasises the need for children to honour their parents, and makes this the fifth commandment (Deut. 5:16). The word 'honour' means 'to prize highly', 'to show respect', 'to glorify and exalt'. It has nuances of caring for and showing affection (Ps. 91:15).[3]

One of the purposes of the command was to enable parents to transmit their faith to the children. In Deuteronomy the fifth commandment is placed in that context. The task of parents is set out in Deuteronomy 4:9f and 6:7, 20f, and in between comes the instruction to honour parents. Parents were to show their children what God was like. On the other side of the coin, a child honoured his parents by carrying into his life the God-like qualities he had learnt from them.

The well-being of society depended on this. That is why the command to honour parents is the only commandment to have the promise attached, 'so that you' (a reference to all the people) 'may live long and that it may go well in the land the Lord your God is giving you' (Deut. 5:16). The first four commandments deal with the people's relationship to God. The fifth wants to continue that relationship from one generation to the next. As this happened, the intended global family would become a godly family.

Why it's important today

Again, this community emphasis is a far cry from modern thought. But it can help children to break free from their parents without hurting them. It provides a reason for honouring parents which is in line with the teenager's need to become independent of them. The command does not say, 'Honour your parents to show that you love them, or to show that you are committed to them, or to enable *them* to have a good life'.

Such a command would put teenagers in an impossible doublebind. It would tie them to their parents when they were trying to break free. It would suggest that they have a primary

---

3. B. S. Childs, *Exodus. A Commentary*, p. 418.

commitment to home when their instinct is to leave home. Sometimes the commandment has been interpreted in this way, and it has left young people confused.

Instead, the command tells children to be committed to God's people in the first instance, not to their parents. They are to keep the law for the sake of God's wider family. The child is to learn about God's people when he is young. As he grows up, he is to decide whether to commit himself to those people. If he chooses to do so, he will look at the world from their point of view.

His first loyalty will not be to his parents, but to God's family. From that perspective he will be able to view critically the life of his parents. They will provide plenty of examples for him to avoid for the sake of God's people! Putting God's family first will channel the teenager's natural inclination to find fault with his home.

But he is not to reject it. The adult child must respect his parents precisely because he now serves a higher loyalty – an allegiance to God's family (of which his parents may be part). For the sake of this family, he must remain committed to them.

In practice that will involve discerning the things of God that he was taught at home, carrying those lessons into his life, and as a mark of respect thanking his parents explicitly for what he learnt from them. ('If we'd never had family prayers, I would never have learnt. . .'; 'Those walks we had together were so worth while because. . .') Parents will feel acknowledged and appreciated, and will be more able to encourage their children in return – affirming them when they become parents for example, instead of criticising.

Honouring also means forgiving your parents, for resentment is a far stronger emotion than respect. An adult who is deeply resentful because he was unfairly treated at home will find it impossible to 'prize highly' or to 'glorify and exalt' his parents. He will need to forgive before he can respect. That will be a major step toward reconciliation at home and the healing of past hurts. In turn, the benefits of this reconciliation will flow into relationships outside the home. Healed families will bring healing to God's people. Honouring parents is good for the community.

Conclusion

Assuming these Old Testament insights are confirmed by the New Testament, how do they relate to some of the family pressures discussed in part 1? In chapter 3 we saw that damaging rules of behaviour are passed down the generations, so that – as the ancient Israelite proverb puts it – 'the fathers have eaten sour grapes and the children's teeth are set on edge'. Chapter 4 suggested that the self-please ethic encourages modern families to hand on rules which encourage rejection or clinging (or both). Old Testament principles would encourage a more healthy pattern of family rules.

First, they would promote acceptance rather than rejection. For a child is unlikely to feel ignored if parents spend time teaching her as Deuteronomy requires; nor is she likely to feel unimportant if they care enough lovingly to discipline her; nor again is she likely to think her views have been belittled if, as she grows up, she is encouraged to make up her own mind. She is much more likely to feel that she matters. Which means she has every chance of growing up to be an accepting mother herself.

Secondly, these Old Testament principles would encourage parents to release their child rather than cling to her. They would encourage parents not only to allow her to become a separate, independent adult, but to avoid manipulating her from an early age. Deuteronomy encourages parents to give good reasons for what they say, which is step one to allowing children to contest what they are being told. Parental values are not to be stuck rigidly to the child with a permanent emotional glue, as in the case of the boy who clings to his parents' views because he is afraid to lose their love. They are to be fixed with a knot of explanation, so that later the child can undo the knot if he chooses.

Thirdly, as we have just seen, by encouraging children to honour their parents, the Old Testament implicitly encourages them to forgive their parents. This will break the chain of resentment that lies behind a lot of family hurt. A mother has been scarred as a child. As an adult, she may unconsciously try to get even with her parents by inflicting pain on members of her own family, and that pattern may be repeated down the generations. But children who 'highly esteem' their parents and so forgive them, can be released from the need to get even.

They will discover that forgiveness is perhaps the most effective family therapy there is.

6

Shining through

On 14 July 1989 television crews from around the world converged on Paris as France celebrated the bicentenary of the storming of the Bastille, traditionally regarded as the outbreak of the French Revolution. The French were rightly proud that the revolution had thrust to the forefront of modern thought the values of liberty, equality and fraternity. However the British Prime Minister, Mrs Thatcher, caused a minor – and distinctly non-fraternal – stir by suggesting that these values had not been invented by the French at all, but by the British.

Perhaps it would come as a surprise to her to discover that these values in fact pre-date not only the French Revolution, but the major landmarks of British history as well – by nearly 2000 years. They are to be found in the Old Testament. Family relationships in ancient Israel were to strain toward equality, solidarity and liberty. And because, as the central unit in society, life revolved around families, as these qualities were displayed in Israelite homes they were to become a distinguishing feature of the nation. As a result, God's glory was to shine through the people.

Now the word 'glory' is seldom used today. But the Old Testament often uses it of God who is said to reveal his glory in Israel (e.g. Isa. 44:23). That means that God's magnificent, resplendent character was to be seen in the life of the nation. This was to happen – in part – when the people's relationships were marked by equality, solidarity and liberty, because these qualities are highly prized by God. So as individual families displayed these virtues, they would help to create not only a national family, but a glorious one.

The ideal

This ideal for family relationships is implied in Genesis 1 – 2, where family relationships also stand for relationships in general. 'Adam' in the Hebrew sounds like 'man'. He represents humanity as a whole. His relationship with Eve, therefore, contains principles not just for marriage, but for the generality of human relationships. The distinction between family and society is blurred. What is to happen in the family is to happen in society. When God's glory is reflected in the family, it will be reflected in the community.

Traditionally it is said that the opening chapters in Genesis teach male authority. The two shall become one flesh – and I am he! So it is suggested that the creation of the woman to help the man implies that she was subordinate to him. However, 'helper' (Gen. 2:18) need not imply subordination. Of the nineteen times the word occurs in the Old Testament, on fifteen occasions it is used with reference to God. The other four times use it of allies (e.g. Isa. 30:5). You can help someone without being under them. Indeed, often it is the stronger person who helps the weaker!

It has also been said that Adam's naming of Eve implies an authority over her. Naming in the ancient Near East was an expression of authority – rather like parents today who assume they have the right to name their child because it belongs to them.

However, in the Old Testament a standard formula was used when someone named a person in a way that denoted authority over them. It involved using two words, the verb 'to call' and the noun 'name' – as in Genesis 4:25, 'she bore a son and called his name Seth'. There is a good example of this formula in Genesis 2, when these words are found together in Adam's naming of the animals; clearly he has authority over them (v. 19).

But when Adam says 'she shall be called "woman" ' in v. 23, he does not use this naming formula. The word 'name' does not appear, and 'woman' is used as a common noun designating gender rather than a proper name. Adam had no intention of calling Eve 'woman' for the rest of her life! Verse 23 is an exclamation of delight, not an expression of authority. The word translated 'woman' may literally mean 'like-opposite him', or possibly even 'matching his eminence'.[1] The man recognised that here was a companion who, unlike anything else he had seen, somehow fell into the same unique category of creation as he did, and was therefore his equal.

This was the ideal that existed before the Fall. It was the basis of the unity that was to exist in human relationships. This unity is strongly implied in Genesis 1:27, where God's image is not given to the man and the woman alone, nor to the man and the woman separately, but to the man and the woman together. It is divided between them as they work in harmony, as a single unit. Together, in relationship, the man and the woman reflect God.

This togetherness is further emphasised in chapter 2. The woman is created explicitly as a companion to the man, so that he would not be alone. They unite to form 'one flesh' (Gen. 2:24). This is the language of solidarity – 'bone of my bones and flesh of my flesh' (v. 23).

Their togetherness was to set the world free. It freed Adam from loneliness. It was to free creation from evil. There are hints that evil was present in the world, even before the Fall. Satan crawls into the garden. God uses a very strong word, 'subdue', when he tells Adam and Eve to master the world. In the Hebrew 'subdue' may well have had the idea of trampling. It seems more likely that they were to stamp on evil than on nature.

God saw that the world was good, but the word 'good' does not necessarily mean perfect. The world was good for the purpose that God had in mind: Adam and Eve in a relationship of equality and solidarity were to give birth to a global family, which would liberate the world from evil and bring out the full potential of creation.

But the Fall prevented all that. It introduced domination into human relationships, which affected the prevailing culture. Families were now given the task, in the midst of their sinfulness, of helping society to pull away from the norms of that fallen culture, back toward the pre-Fall ideal.

The Old Testament reflects many of the cultural assumptions of the day. The man was legally to own his wife, for example (Exod. 21:3, 22). Yet it hints too at principles which can be

---

1. I am grateful to the Revd Dr David Atkinson for pointing out to me the possible translations.

said to reflect God's will because, as we shall see, unlike many of the cultural practices of ancient Israel, they are endorsed by the New Testament. These principles also had the potential to undermine ancient culture in the long term. God started where families were in order to lead them into something new. They were to help create a society which reflected God's glory.

The search for equality

This was one of the tasks of marriage. Now some people have said that the ideal of equality between husband and wife no longer applied once humanity had sinned. They have taken God's punishment on Eve, 'Your desire will be for your husband, and he will rule over you' (Gen. 3:16) as a statement of what ought to happen.

But it is not an 'ought' statement at all. It is a prediction, a 'will be' statement. God is describing what will happen as a result of sin. The woman will turn toward her husband, and the man will use that dependence to rule over her. The prediction is strikingly confirmed in Genesis 3:20, after God has passed judgement. Adam asserts his authority by employing the standard naming formula to call his wife Eve. It was the first time that that formula had been applied to a human being.

The word normally translated 'desire' in Genesis 3:16 actually means 'turning', and is translated that way in the earliest Greek version of the Old Testament, the Septuagint. The sense of the verse becomes, 'Your turning will be toward your husband, and he will rule over you.' There may be a hint that having turned away from God, the woman turns (for security perhaps?) to her husband instead. She finds herself dependent on the man rather than being dependent on God.

Clearly she is not to stay in that position. The whole pattern of Scripture encourages women and men to turn back to God. Perhaps an implication of Genesis 3:16 is that if the woman's turning stops being toward her husband, if she ceases to depend on him and turns back to God instead, she can restore the Genesis 1 – 2 ideal of a more equal relationship.[2]

This ideal is celebrated in the Song of Songs, where male

---

2. Walter C. Kaiser, Jr., *Toward Old Testament Ethics*. Academic Books, Grand Rapids 1983, pp. 204–6.

dominance and sexual stereotyping are entirely absent. The woman actively seeks the man for love-making (3:1ff). She is an independent person who keeps vineyards and pastures flocks (1:6, 8). Equality and harmony are expressed in the formula, 'My husband is mine and I am his' (2:16, 6:3).

The woman's statement, 'I belong to my lover and his desire is for me' (7:10), neatly reverses the prediction of Genesis 3:16 that her 'desire will be for your husband, and he will rule over you.' The Song implies that God's statement of what will happen after the Fall is not irreversible. Couples who depend on God can recapture something of the idyllic relationship which existed before humanity sinned.

There are hints of this elsewhere in the Old Testament. In Proverbs 2:17, for example, the word 'partner' is used of husbands. That is a term which the Israelites reserved for the closest of friends. Suggesting that the wife was in partnership or close friendship with her husband was a far cry from the ancient idea of wife as chattel and child-bearer, but not companion.

Whereas inequality can lead to oppression which stifles people, equality releases people to be more fully themselves. That seems to have been the case with the 'ideal wife' in Proverbs 31. Nothing is said about male headship, but she is certainly not oppressed by her husband! She is free to pursue a bewildering variety of business and household activities (vv. 13, 16 etc.). With extraordinary energy, she makes forays into traditionally male preserves. Her 'male' business activities are as important as her 'female' domestic ones.

By doing these things, the wife ensured that her family made an impact on the community. She supported the needy (Prov. 31:20), she increased trade which benefited the economy (vv. 16, 24) and she freed the head of the house to take part in local politics (v. 23). Equality within the home will affect the wider society.

Equality was not totally lost sight of as far as relationships with children were concerned. We saw in the last chapter how it was expected that adult children should reach their own spiritual conclusions and become emotionally independent of their parents. This pulled against the immense authority invested in Middle Eastern fathers. Their authority was to be by no means absolute.

The overall picture is of family members striving toward

equality. Husbands and wives achieve this today when they are flexible in their roles, when the man's interests do not automatically come first and when they share the decision-making fairly. Parents promote equality when they give steadily more responsibility to their children as they mature.

The search for solidarity

Lord Hailsham once described marriage as 'a set of interlocking dictatorships'. The Old Testament on the other hand sees it as a single unit pulling in one direction. Families were to promote solidarity. An intimate relationship between a man and a woman is set out as the ideal, despite the practice of polygamy (King Solomon had 700 wives!). God seems to have accepted the polygamy of some of the godly men of Israel not because it was desirable in itself, but as a concession to the prevailing culture.

The Old Testament hints at a better way. The ideal of 'oneness' in a monogamous marriage is reflected in the Genesis 2:24 idea of husband and wife cleaving to each other. The Song of Songs speaks of the man and woman belonging very closely to one another (2:16; 6:3; 7:10). It expects their love to last (8:7; cf. Deut. 5:18).

Indeed, the Song's exquisite celebration of love, in which the couple are entirely wrapped up with each other, only makes sense if the author expected marriage to be exclusive. The Song may in fact have been a call to reject polygamy in favour of a higher ideal.

Proverbs 1:8f tells both parents to instruct their children, and it assumes that they speak with one voice. 'They' (plural) will be a 'garland' (singular) on the child's head (cf. Prov. 6:20). There is a further hint in the command to honour father *and* mother. Both are to be respected, together, as a unit. In other words, children were not to be allowed to side with one parent against the other.

This solidarity extended to others in the family. Typically the sons would work the land together, often supervised by their father. The farm was regarded as a family business and was effectively owned by the family (in contrast to the Canaanite city states where all land was owned by the king). Various laws existed to prevent families from permanently selling off their land (e.g. Lev. 25:8ff). If observed, these laws would have greatly strengthened the family as a unit. Its common interest in the land would have drawn its members together.

So would the custom of *go'el*. If there was a risk of family property being sold off, a near relative – known as the *go'el* – was to buy it back on behalf of the family (Lev. 25:25ff). Land was normally a household's main source of livelihood. If a sizeable plot was sold, the farm might become too small to support the family. Sooner or later members of the household would have to work for someone else. When harvests were poor, there was a danger that these labourers would be left destitute because they were no longer required. There was no redundancy pay in Israel! If a hired worker lost his job, he lost everything. By encouraging a relative to buy the property before it went to someone else, the *go'el* preserved the family's economic independence.

The *go'el* also covered situations where the family had become so impoverished that a member had to be sold into slavery – to raise the cash to pay off the family's debts for example. When that happened, the *go'el* was to buy back the relative who had been sold as a slave and restore his freedom (Lev. 25:47ff). The custom of *go'el* was an expression of family solidarity, therefore. Members would stand by each other if they got into trouble.

This could be seen as a drain on family resources: the family would be spending money on those who were in difficulty. But equally it was an investment in the future. Those saved from hardship would be indebted to relatives who had helped them. They (or their immediate kin) might be expected to do a good turn when others needed help to realise their potential. The character of the nation would be affected. It would be a society in which people were cared for.

In our individualistic age, it is easy to forget how committed people can be to a group. Yet supporters will travel miles to follow 'their' football team. New York teenagers will take great risks to protect the reputation of 'their' gang. Yorkshire miners will take very different risks to protect 'their' community from pit closures. Israelites were to be even more loyal to 'their' family.

Cities have been defined as lots of people being lonely together. Israel was to consist of households where people belonged together. There was to be a homely 'feel' to the nation. That belonging is not inconsistent with city life today. In some areas of high unemployment where the extended family still flourishes, families operate as single units.

So the earnings of someone in paid work are shared around to provide a cushion for members without jobs. Cars are loaned, small sums exchange hands, an employed son may ensure his unemployed father has the price of a pint at the end of the week. Opportunities for casual work are shared round the family. If a young mother gets a job in the launderette, relatives will mind the children. Solidarity can still work.[3]

The search for liberty

The *go'el* highlights the third way that families were to reflect God's glory. The purpose of the *go'el* was to protect liberty. The family's economic freedom was preserved when it was able to hang on to its land. It remained an independent farming unit instead of depending on others for work. Likewise, obviously, the slave's liberty was restored when the *go'el* bought his freedom.

Families were also to bring liberty to outsiders nearby. They were to protect the disadvantaged. Land was to be cultivated so that part of the crop was left for foreigners temporarily living in Israel, and for orphans and widows (Deut. 24:19ff). These were people who were living outside families, and could not get a livelihood from the land because property was held on a family basis. Families were to guarantee them freedom from starvation.

Foreign slaves in an Israelite home found that it could be a route to emancipation. Slaves could share their master's inheritance (Prov. 17:2) and even succeed in the absence of heirs (Gen. 15:3). One slave married his master's daughter (1 Chron. 2:34f).

The family was to preserve freedom in society at large. Two elements which made the Old Testament unique in the ancient Near East were its abhorrence of class distinctions and of a centralised state. As originally envisaged, economic power was to be decentralised: it was to be located in extended families.

That is why the main source of livelihood in Israel, land, was

---

3. Michael Moynagh, *Making Unemployment Work*. Tring 1985, p. 24.

divided as widely as possible between extended families, and why various laws encouraged families to hold on to their land rather than sell it. Otherwise a gap would have emerged between rich families who could afford to buy and poor households who were forced to sell. Gradually these rich families would have accumulated more and more wealth, till they were in a position to exploit families who had sold their land.

The family was to be a bastion against the concentration of political, as well as economic power. As the central economic unit, it was natural that the family should have an important political role. Originally political power in Israel was decentralised and based on a wide network of local elders, who were the heads of extended families.

If families had hung on to this power, they would have encouraged economic and political freedom. They would have prevented the state accumulating steadily more influence at their expense. But instead, as we shall see, the representatives of the extended families chose to give up their power. They asked for a king.

They were warned that under a king families would be oppressed. Children would be separated from their parents and press-ganged into royal service. Families would be forced to sell their best land to the king (1 Sam. 8:10ff). But families ignored the warning – and the result was that many *were* exploited (e.g. 1 Kings 12:1ff; Neh. 5:1ff).

The family was to be a means of liberation from evil in general. It was through a family act of worship – the Passover – that Israelites escaped the death of their first-born, the plague which finally convinced Pharaoh to set the Israelites free. The Passover, which remained a family meal despite Deuteronomy 16:2, celebrated each year Israel's liberation from Egypt.

It was largely through family worship that the nation was to be kept loyal to the Lord, and to experience the economic and political freedom that were to have been the fruits of this loyalty. For the first two commandments, prohibiting false gods and idolatry, applied not only to corporate acts of worship by the whole community: they had a very particular reference to families.

Worship, it seems, was located very much in the home. When Jacob fled from his father-in-law, Laban, Rachel (his second wife) stole her father's *household* gods (Gen. 31:19). To give David a chance to escape from Saul his wife, Michal, hid a domestic idol in his bed (1 Sam. 19:13). It seems to have been the custom for images of false gods to be worshipped on a day-to-day basis within the family. Visits to public centres of worship, though important, were less frequent. Deuteronomy envisages only periodic visits to the one true centre of worship, the Jerusalem temple.

The call to pure worship, therefore, was a summons in the first instance to families. This was emphasised by the promise that failure to keep the second commandment would result in punishment of the extended family. God would punish 'the children for the sin of the fathers to the third and fourth generation' (Exod. 20:5). The Old Testament scholar, G. A. F. Knight, comments:

> In Moses' day, as in ours throughout the Third World, all four generations of the one family lived together in the one village, even under one roof. Thus it is inevitable that if the headman 'commits adultery' with a foreign god. . . his grandchildren and even his great-grandchildren living with him are bound to experience the penalty of his disloyalty. 'A drunken captain creates an undisciplined crew'. There is therefore no question of God punishing children as yet unborn. . . God's judgement on apostasy remains *within the family group*.[4]

Families were to worship the one God without using idols. If they did this they would be free to enjoy the opportunities that prosperity would bring, and they would be free from foreign oppression. But if they worshipped God falsely, the nation's economic and political liberty would be taken away (Deut. 28:1ff). The ten commandments start on this note because family (as well as community) worship was the key to national liberty.

Poverty and oppression are so complex today that it is hard for families to imagine how they can make a difference. So it is perhaps comforting that Israelite families were not expected to act on an heroic scale. They were to order their lives in small things – in protecting relatives who fell on hard times, in how they treated their slaves and harvested the fields, in just

---

4. George A. F. Knight, *Theology as Narration: A Commentary on the Book of Exodus*. Handsell, Edinburgh 1976, pp. 136–7. It is worth noting that the command to observe the sabbath is also aimed directly at families. Deuteronomy 5:14 addresses the heads of families.

being there as a viable farming unit, in worshipping God at home as well as in the temple. If all families had done that, the national whole would have been much larger than the sum of its parts.

There are many little things which modern families can do. They can avoid wasting resources in their homes. They can protect the environment outside their front doors. They can use their money to protect people in need. They can join other families in their neighbourhood to request – or organise – better children's facilities, a bereavement call-in centre or more support for carers of dependent relatives. By worshipping together, the family can meet God in prayer.

The shortest horror story in the world is this:

> 'What happens to women who marry dull men?
> They go into the suburbs and never come out again.'[5]

But families need not be like that – vacuums without meaning. Just being there committed to equality, solidarity and liberty can make an immense difference to people round about. Israelite families were at the heart of society, and as a person's heart affects his or her life, so families were to determine the quality of Israel's life.

Families can still affect society today – by just being there. Spouses who are committed to equality will make sure that they have an equal chance to develop their gifts. The 'ideal wife' in Proverbs took her abilities into the community. Partners who release each other will find that their abilities touch the lives of neighbours and friends, too. Being there makes a difference.

Families who are committed to solidarity will not allow an uncle, through alcoholism, to sink into destitution, uncared for. Nor will they allow their children to become vandals by roaming the streets unsupervised. They will stand by one another, and not leave it to society to pick up the pieces. Being there makes a difference.

Families who are committed to liberty will be concerned about the narrowing of opportunities in their streets and in their neighbourhoods. They will become involved in activities

---

5. Peter Vardy, *And if it's true?* Marshall Pickering, Basingstoke, 1988, p. 39.

which free people from need – in fostering a child, in helping to finance a crèche for single mothers, in organising a social for elderly people living on their own, in praying for the neighbourhood as a family. They will know that being there, in these little things, makes a difference.

This is not to say that government and other institutions don't have important roles as well. Yet even so, as families pursue equality, solidarity and liberty, they will confront often in small, sometimes in larger ways some of the social pressures in chapter 2. Instead of women being on the edge of the family, in terms of status, spouses will seek to create a more equal partnership. Instead of some families being on the edge of community, isolated and vulnerable, the attempt by other families to build community will make newcomers feel they belong. Where families are on the edge of prosperity, the commitment of other families to freedom from need will lead to some amelioration of poverty. Even in places where everyone is poor, families which share the little they have will still be of help to those who are worst off.

Albert Einstein once said, 'Our world is characterised by an abundance of means, but a shortage of goals.' Old Testament families were to employ an abundance of small means to help achieve a wonderful goal – the creation of God's glorious family.

PART THREE
Enabled families

7

Family despair

Anne Jenkins has helped to pioneer the New Parent Infant Network, Newpin, a London organisation which supports women who have difficulties with their young children. 'Giving someone a sense of their own self-worth makes the problem much less of a nagging anxiety,' she declares. 'What happens in an abusing situation is that the shame of doing it makes you deny that it goes on; it's too painful – you forget how hard, or how many times you did it.'[1]

Through Newpin, mothers meet people who are in similar situations or have done things just as bad. They realise that they are not the only ones to have failed, and they feel better. They stop thinking that they are worse than everyone else. They start to gain confidence. They are then more willing to face up to what they have done and to learn how to change.

There must be very few families which don't have skeletons hidden away. As a clergyman I am sometimes amazed how, time and again, when I get to know an outwardly normal and healthy family, I find tucked out of sight mistakes which the family finds deeply embarrassing. I am amazed, that is, till I remember that my family is just the same.

Knowing that other families have blown it just like yours is a great encouragement. It is specially encouraging, perhaps, to notice the endless stream of family disasters in the Old Testament, despite the gulf between its world and ours.

Here were a people with a special relationship with God, in touch with him directly through the numerous prophets who were part of their everyday life. They had profound insight into God's character which they recorded beautifully in the Psalms and had first-hand experience of God's power through his dramatic and repeated intervention in their lives. Their laws

1. *The Independent*, 10 April 1989.

and institutions had been shaped by God himself. If ever there were people in a position to know the Lord's mind and with an incentive to obey his will, surely it was ancient Israel. Perhaps no nation in the whole of history had so much potential to create healthy families on God-given lines. Yet family failure was endemic – so much so that the well-being of the nation itself was jeopardised.

The next few pages describe how Israelite families failed to create fully the global, God-loving and glorious family that the Lord intended. The following two chapters show how God has intervened to create that family himself. Then in part 4 we shall see how the creation of God's family by God has enabled human families to contribute to it more effectively. God has given human families an important part to play in building his global family. It is a joint enterprise, made possible by the Lord.

Failure to create a global family

The book of Judges contains an extraordinarily brutal story which highlights the link between the health of the family and the health of society. It is about a religious man, a Levite, who has several wives. One of them is treated so badly that she does what is socially unthinkable: she returns home.

The Levite wants her back. So he goes to her father, some distance away, who entertains him royally. Perhaps he wants to placate the man, knowing that by custom his daughter should not have run away. The Levite stays one night, then another, then another. . . Each time he makes to leave, his wife begs him to stay another night. Maybe she only feels safe with her husband if her father is nearby.

At last she can delay no longer. She is forced to leave with her husband. That night they reach the Benjamite town of Gibeah. According to custom, they wait in the market square for someone to offer hospitality, but no one does. Eventually an older man, from the same tribe as the Levite, takes them in.

The evening is interrupted by a violent pounding on the front door. The local residents are demanding to have sex with the Levite. The host suggests that they take the man's wife instead, and the Levite – who was not one to make a sacrifice when someone else could do it just as well – readily agrees. The woman is raped all through the night and left by the front door, dead.

Next morning the Levite steps nonchalantly out of the house. He trips over his wife, but does not realise that she is dead. Far from expressing any concern, he orders her to get up; they are on their way. As soon as he spots that she is dead, however, he is outraged. He cuts her body into pieces and sends the bits to the tribes of Israel, calling on them to avenge the savagery by marching on Benjamin. Civil war ensues, and with difficulty the Benjamites are defeated.

Now this gruesome story contains a significant progression of thought. Evil in the home spreads outward to contaminate the whole nation. First there is a breakdown in family relationships, arising directly from the husband's abuse of his wife. The woman leaves her husband and is reluctant to return. Next, the journey home creates an opportunity for evil to be committed by a tribe. The Benjamites abuse and murder the woman. Finally the evil affects the entire nation. Rather than helping to build a community which would become a global family, the Levite's household provokes a civil war which threatens society.[2] This is a macabre example of what a potent force families could be in preventing Israel becoming the international family God intended.

Deuteronomy 13:6ff highlights the danger. It warns against being enticed by relatives to worship foreign gods – the emotional closeness of families made it particularly easy for members to lead each other astray. The problem with foreign gods was this: the global family God wanted was to be very distinctive. It was to reflect God's character, as we saw in the last two chapters. This was to be a means by which foreigners discovered God's love. As they converted to Israel's God, they would either be drawn into the nation by taking up residence within Israel itself, as in the case of Ruth, or, like Nineveh which turned to the Lord in response to Jonah, they would have an affinity with Israel by acknowledging its God: they would become part of its religious family. In either case they would forsake the most offensive aspects of their culture, and move closer to the religious culture of Israel.

---

2. Susan Niditch, 'The "Sodomite" Theme in Judges 19–20. Family, Community and Social Disintegration', pp. 365–78.

However, if the Israelites were to start worshipping the gods of the surrounding nations, the reverse would happen. Instead of bringing outsiders into their religious culture, the Israelites would end up leaving their culture behind and adopting one from abroad. God's unique world-wide family would be destroyed.

Largely because of individual families, that is precisely what happened. First, when the Israelites occupied the land they refused to drive out the local people, the Canaanites, as commanded by the Lord. They got caught in a snare by adopting Canaanite religion (Judg. 2:1ff). The snare tightened its grip when they started to marry the Canaanites (Judg. 3:5ff). The men could not resist the women, but the closeness of family ties meant that they could not resist the women's gods, either. The marital bond produced spiritual bondage.

The decisive point came under King Solomon. During his reign Israel reached the peak of its influence. His rule stretched from the Euphrates in the north to near Egypt in the south, from the Mediterranean to the Arabian desert. It was the dominant power in the Middle East. Foreign kings brought their adulation – and their tribute. With all Solomon's household articles made of gold and gold lavishly plastered around the temple (1 Kings 10:21; 7:48ff), this was literally Israel's golden age. The nation's wealth was fantastic (1 Kings 10:27).

But Solomon married foreign wives. If the book of Kings is to be believed, he had 700 of them and 300 concubines (1 Kings 11:3). No wonder they led him astray! 'As Solomon grew old, his wives turned his heart after other gods' (1 Kings 11:4). The Lord's reaction was to punish Solomon by encouraging a rebellion of the ten northern tribes. The kingdom was divided into two weaker nations, which lost many of their territories and much of their wealth. Instead of becoming a single global family, thanks to the behaviour of a royal family, events had moved in the opposite direction.

Intermarriage became such a feature of Israelite society that the people were unable to escape the influence of foreign gods (e.g. 1 Kings 16:31ff; Neh. 13:23ff; Mal. 2:11). The result was that the northern kingdom was punished with permanent exile, and the southern kingdom followed suit for seventy years. Instead of families drawing the world into a single family, this special family had got drawn into the world.

Christian homes know how hard it is to avoid being drawn

into the world. They are enticed by the gods of modern society – gods which provide a framework for interpreting life every bit as powerful as the ancient gods. We saw in chapter 2 how work can provide status, purpose, achievement, a 'life-script' and community, all of which were provided by traditional religion. These rewards can be so compelling that they drag people away from home and away from spiritual commitment. Work can become a substitute for family and for God. It can prevent families drawing the world into God's family.

Failure to create a Godly family

'No explanation! There never was.' That was the kind of home in which Michele Guinness, a modern Jewess, grew up.

> You could be as ignorant about your religion as you chose, reject whatever ritual you found tiresome, never attend the synagogue, as long as you had that elusive, indescribable feel for the Jewish way of life. Tradition mattered more than piety. . . 'This Jewish law,' I used to think, 'I can't work it out. Is it just something adults impose on children to spoil all their fun? Can you grow out of it?'[3]

It would be dangerous to project Michele's experience back 3000 years. But one can't help wondering if 'No explanation!' was true of many ancient Israelite parents, and if this was one reason for their repeated failure to pass on a living faith to the next generation. Parents would experience a surge of religious enthusiasm, but time and again this would not get handed down to the children.

Was this the fault of parenting – that parents failed to teach their children about God in the context of love and discipline, as described in chapter 5? Did tradition eventually take over from enthusiasm, so that parents passed on a faith that was hollow and unattractive, with 'no explanations'? Or was it a problem with children – that they refused to honour their parents? We don't know, but whatever the reason it is clear that the chain of faith between generations was regularly broken. This became an important reason for Israel's failure to create an international family loyal to God.

3. Michele Guinness, *Child of the Covenant*. London 1985, p. 45.

In the Genesis story this all begins when Adam and Eve refused to honour their heavenly Father. Eve distrusted him. She preferred to believe the serpent's claim that, contrary to what God had said, she would not die if she ate the fruit (Gen. 3:4). Adam and Eve's rebellion had an immediate effect on their marriage. Their carefree nakedness before the Fall pointed to a transparent harmony, complete intimacy, within their relationship. That had now gone. They wanted to make clothes because they wanted to put up the barriers. An emotional distance had come between them. Adam blamed his wife (Gen. 3:7ff).

There is a profound truth here. Generational conflict is a major source of marital conflict. Adam and Eve were afraid they would be rejected by their Father – that he would punish them because they had sinned. So they became anxious, and that anxiety damaged the marriage. Modern psychology knows only too well how children's relationships to their parents affect their later marriages. Perhaps that is why, as we shall see, Scripture puts such an emphasis on the parent–child relationship. If this relationship is healthy, marriages will be healthy.

Cain is the first father in the Bible to fail totally to pass on knowledge of God to his children. After killing his brother Abel, he is punished by being made a restless wanderer; he will find no place like home (Gen. 4:12, 14). He leaves the Lord's presence, verse 16, and then promptly (v. 17) his wife conceives Enoch. The contrast with Eve's conception of Seth, in verse 25, is stark. Eve acknowledges God's authority by recognising that God has given her the child. Cain has a son after going away from God.

As a wanderer Cain is massively insecure. He is rootless. His only protection against death is the knowledge that if someone does kill him, he will be avenged seven times (by which time it will be too late!) (v. 15). Yet Cain refuses to turn back to God and seek security in him. He tries to create his own security. He builds a city (v. 17). He wants the city to become home, and to give him the safety and sense of belonging he craves.[4]

Far from being taught about God therefore, his children see a father who builds a life without God. The results are disastrous. Cain had succumbed to violence, but his descendant,

---

4. J. Ellul, *The Meaning of the City*, pp. 5–6.

Lamech, exults in it (v. 23f). Successive generations have moved steadily further from the Lord.

One family, however, does remain loyal to God. Eve gives birth to Seth and recognises that he is a gift from God. Seth also has a son, and 'at that time men began to call upon the name of the Lord' (v. 26). This has been seen as the beginning of the story of God's people, who become Israel. How good were they at passing on the faith, baton-like, from one generation to another?

'Not very' is the Bible's answer. One of the themes of the Book of Judges is how one generation turns back to God, and – repeatedly – the next turns away again. The generation conflict was known in Scripture long before it was discovered in the West! It is summed up in the story of Samson.

The story is recorded because Samson stands for Israel. His parents accept the Nazirite regulations, which represent God's covenant with Israel, and keep them just as the 'fathers' of the people had kept the covenant (2:22). But Samson falls away like Israel does. He breaks his Nazirite vows by eating from a dead and impure animal and by cutting his hair (14:8ff; 16:17ff); he marries a foreign woman who leads him astray. Samson is captured by the Philistines, just as the people are punished by being handed over to their enemies (2:14). Samson finally repents, again like Israel, but as the rest of Judges implies, the cycle will be repeated all over again.[5]

And so it happens – not only in the Book of Judges. Spiritual giants like Eli, Samuel and David all have sons who turn from God. Ordinary families were no better. It seems that Israelite homes, like modern ones, were chronically unable to create a community which persistently loved God. Instead of passing God's laws from one generation to the next, destructive rules like those we discussed in chapter 3 get handed down.

Maybe when we feel burdened by our family failures, we can take comfort from the fact that Old Testament families, often greatly used by God, were little better.

---

5. Edward L. Greenstein, 'The Riddle of Samson', pp. 237–60.

Failure to create a glorious family

It is not unusual for a person's life to be crowned with disappointment. That was certainly the case with Samuel. His had been a long life, in which he had risen to the very top of Israelite society. After years in that position, and feeling the effect of advancing age, he had delegated the task of upholding justice and maintaining national security to his sons. But they had run amok, proving thoroughly corrupt and antagonising the elders – the heads of the extended families. It was these elders who asked Samuel to appoint a king.

It was obvious that Samuel's sons had turned from God (1 Sam. 8:3). It seems that the rest of their generation had done so too. The request for a king came from their contemporaries – the elders refer to Samuel, but not to themselves, as being old in verse 5, which suggests that they belonged to the same generation as his sons. The Lord saw this request as the rejection of himself. Once again there was spiritual conflict between the generations. Samuel's contemporaries had turned to the Lord (7:2ff), but their sons had turned away again.

Samuel warns that the introduction of monarchy would oppress *families*. The king would break up the family unit by conscripting sons into his army and daughters into his household. He would take the best land from families, and tax them so heavily that the household-and-farm would no longer be a viable unit. Families would lose their economic independence (8:11ff). Monarchy would centralise economic and political power at the expense of families.

But the heads of the extended families ignore Samuel's advice. They have turned from God, so they are not willing to rely on him for security. They want a king instead. And they are prepared to give up their power to get one. This is perhaps the turning-point in Israel's history. Families abandon their position as bulwarks against oppression, as defenders of political and economic freedom. The Lord, who respects their will, gives them a king, but the rest of Israel's history would show how appallingly and viciously accurate Samuel's prediction was. Kingship would destroy kinship.

An encouragement for families

Israelite families failed to create a global family because instead of encouraging outsiders to share their religious culture, outsiders – through intermarriage – drew the people away from their culture. They failed to create a godly family because Israelite homes proved woefully unable to pass on the faith from one generation to the next. They failed to create a glorious family, because by surrendering their power to the king they gave up the power to protect freedom and justice within the nation.

As modern families look at these failures, dare they claim to have done much better? Just as Israelite families came to be oppressed by forces in their society, we have seen how society damages the modern home. The place of work and of women, the lack of community and of wealth, have all left their scars on the family. We have also seen how a chain of injustice is passed frequently from one generation to another, as families become trapped by self-perpetuating rules. The self-please ethic has proved too weak to prevent family members treating each other unfairly.

Yet the failure of Israelite families is not without comfort. There were notable exceptions. The existence in each generation of people who loved God suggests that families had at least some success in passing on the faith. There is the lovely story of Ruth. And then there is the story of David's family.

For a start David slept with the woman next door, Bathsheba, and arranged for her husband to be killed so that he could marry her. He exercised no control over his children. His eldest son, Amnon, was allowed to rape his half-sister and get away with it. The next eldest, Absalom, had Amnon murdered and got off with a light punishment.

Absalom then led a rebellion against his father. Perhaps that was the result of David being away so much, on countless military expeditions, while Absalom was young; maybe the boy grew up nursing a fierce resentment against his father, which exploded into open revolt. More was to come. The next son rebelled against his father too. This time the rebellion was explicitly linked to lack of discipline at home (1 Kings 1:6). David was an unfaithful husband, a disastrous father and his children were appalling rebels.

Those of us who are disappointed by our families and know

how badly we have failed, how we have betrayed our spouses and neglected our children, can take comfort from knowing that David was just as bad, if not worse. Yet the Bible presents him as a model king. Despite his failures, God still used him. Moreover God chose to work in *his* family, gradually refining it over the years, till eventually it produced a home ready to raise the Messiah. And it was through the Messiah that God established the global, godly and glorious family that Israelite households had failed to create.

So Israelite families were not total failures at all! As a nation, they had begun the work of building God's family by providing a suitable home in which Jesus could be raised and an appropriate society in which he could live. Yet on their own they had been totally unable to complete the task. It needed the Messiah, through the cross, to enable human families to contribute more fully to God's family. Jesus did not found a family: he found the beginnings of one, and made it possible for it to be made complete.

David's family shows that no family is too bad for God. Not even family failure – whether in the ancient world or the modern one – is too bad for God. For God is stronger than families. He can use them. He can save them. There can be hope in all homes which despair.

8

Family deliverance

The young girl was excited about her speech and drama competition. She pleaded with her father to come and watch. But no, he was far too busy. When the afternoon came and she was about to do her piece, she saw the door open and her father creep into the back of the hall. He had changed his mind. Thrilled, she tried to make even more of an impression.

Though she did not win a prize, she knew she had done very well (there were many entrants). All she needed to make her day was for her father to say how proud he was of her. She approached him in eager expectation, only to hear, 'But why didn't you win?' Her face told its story: the agony and disappointment of yet another rejection. Whatever she did, however hard she tried, Dad was never satisfied.

Rejection must be the most basic of all family hurts. Whatever pain a person feels in his or her home, it always boils down to some form of rejection. Even when relatives cling to each other, in a way that seems to be the opposite of rejection, what they are really doing is rejecting each other's autonomy. They are rejecting one another's right to be themselves.

As we turn to the New Testament, we shall see that God has overcome human failure to create fully his family. Despite their shortcomings, he has made it possible for families to help more effectively build his family. The starting point is the cross, through which the Father and Son entered the human experience of rejection so as to bring healing to families. They were able to do this because Jesus became a man.

A model home

Jesus' home in Nazareth provides a link between the Old Testament and the New. For in producing a home fit for the Messiah,

Israelite families share in the achievement of Jesus in making possible the full creation of God's family. From the little we know, the upbringing which equipped Jesus for his task provides a model of parent–child relationships that comes very close to the Old Testament ideal.

Apart from his birth and the events surrounding it, there are only four stories in the Bible about Jesus' relationship to his parents. The first tells how at the age of twelve he had been brought to the temple to celebrate the Passover. It seems that his family had travelled in a large group of friends and relatives. So it was natural that on the way home, Joseph and Mary should assume that Jesus was with friends elsewhere in the group.

In fact, Jesus had stayed behind in the temple where he was talking to the theologians. They were amazed by his grasp of the law, and it seems by his questions. Just as in Deuteronomy it had been assumed that parents would raise questioning children, so we find Jesus questioning the experts (Luke 2:46f). Joseph and Mary had brought Jesus up not only to know the law, but to ask questions about it, as the Old Testament required.

At the same time Jesus was beginning to separate from his parents. He was starting to own the faith for himself. That was why he was deep in conversation. Perhaps he was checking out what his parents had told him to make sure it was true; maybe he was asking the questions that his parents could not answer! Whatever it was, he was doing his own research so that he could reach his own conclusions. His faith would not be shaped by his parents alone, a pale imitation of theirs. It would have its own unique shape, moulded by the results of *his* enquiries.

So when his parents eventually find their son, and Mary with a mother's natural concern reprimands him for having gone off on his own, Jesus replies with startling originality, 'Why were you searching for me? Didn't you know I had to be in my father's house?' (v. 49).

The resident scholars, who knew their Old Testament backwards, must have been astonished. In all the long biblical record no prophet or priest, neither king nor commoner, not even Moses who built the tabernacle, nor David who planned the temple, nor Solomon who actually built it, no one had ever referred to the tabernacle or temple as 'my father's house'.

FAMILY DELIVERANCE

Jesus was aware of an intimacy with God that no one had experienced before.

That is why he could address God as 'Abba', a very intimate term which comes close to 'Daddy'. He knew that he was totally and unconditionally loved by his Father. This gave him a unique sense of belonging to his Father. And that sense of belonging convinced Jesus that his loyalty must be ultimately to his heavenly Father rather than to his earthly parents. He was the Father's Son before he was his parents' boy. His question to Mary was a gentle way of pointing that out.

This conviction that God came first in his life, not his parents, was made clear to Mary when Jesus was an adult. Jesus was teaching a crowd of people inside a house. Mary and his brothers arrived at the front door, and sent in a message to say that they were there. Jesus replied to the effect, 'Who are my mother and my brothers? Look at this crowd here. They're my real family' (Mark 3:31ff).

Jesus knew that the people round him would be with him in heaven (along with Mary and his brothers, it later became clear). They were his true family, because like him they would belong to his Father. By totally identifying with this family, his Father's family, Jesus showed that his dependence on earthly parents had been broken completely.

Mary must have found this quite painful. It seems that she had not yet released her son and was still trying to control his movements. Mark 3:21 can have various translations, but there is good reason to think that the NIV is close to the mark.[1] Jesus and his disciples were so busy with the crowd that they did not have time to eat. 'When his family heard about this, they went to take charge of him, for they said, "He is out of his mind." ' Mary still wanted to mother Jesus by making sure that he was properly fed.

At the wedding of Cana she appears to be doing something similar. Behind her comment to Jesus, 'They have no more wine', we sense the interference of a mother who is over-anxious that Jesus should do something. His reaction, 'Dear woman, why do you involve me? My time has not yet come', seems to contain a plea that he be given space – that he be allowed to act in his own (or in God's) time.

Eventually Mary stopped interfering. She allowed him his

---

1. Raymond E. Brown et al, *Mary in the New Testament*, pp. 54–9.

freedom. If her son chose to go without food for a while, or to take his time about things, that was up to him. Indeed, so completely did she let go that by the end of his life Jesus could regard her as one of his followers (who were dependent on him). He asked his disciple, John, to look after her and described them both as members of the same family. Mary was to be John's mother and John her son (John 19:26f). Mary had become one of Jesus' disciples.

Mary's relationship with her son was no longer based on him following her, but on her submitting to him. She had reached that point of totally releasing her son which many older parents experience, when age forces them to depend on and in some ways submit to their children. Mary had learnt to be dependent on Jesus.

Jesus' separation from his parents did not mean that he stopped honouring them. It is significant that at the end of the temple incident, while Jesus was a boy, we are explicitly told that Jesus went with his parents and was obedient to them (Luke 2:51). On the cross, at the most excruciating moment of his life, Jesus was still honouring his mother – not through a form of childish obedience, but by providing for her welfare. He made sure that she was cared for by handing her over to John. Perhaps it is significant that at the moment Jesus had become most independent, we read of him returning his mother's love.

So it was that Jesus' upbringing equipped him for his work – to save that global family which human families had been unable to create on their own. His parents had carried out their teaching function, Jesus had separated from them, and yet he continued to honour them. Knowledge of God had been handed from one generation to the next. The cross ensured that it would be passed on to all generations.

A suffering family

When I work with people on the edge of the church, I find that what often confuses them most is the Trinity. The formula developed by the early church, 'three persons, one substance', doesn't mean an awful lot today!

More recently, some theologians have suggested that the unity of the Father, Son and Holy Spirit is like the oneness

FAMILY DELIVERANCE

that can occur in human relationships. In marriage, for instance, 'they are no longer two, but one' (Matt. 19:6). Similarly, the three persons of the Trinity are united by the intimacy of their fellowship: they have a common mind and a common will.

This way of looking at the Trinity focuses on the relationships within it. One theologian who has explored this is a German called Jurgen Moltmann. In 1976 Moltmann caused quite a stir when he published an important book, *The Crucified God*. In it he looked at what happened to the relationships between the Father, Son and Holy Spirit when Jesus died on the cross. He suggested that the cross involved suffering not only by Jesus, but also by the Father. The Son felt forsaken by the Father, while the Father felt the pain of seeing his Son as a rebel and witnessing his death.[2] This opens interesting possibilities for a theology of the family. May it not be that at the crucifixion the Father and Son experienced some of the core hurts of human parents and children?

Some critics however said that Moltmann had gone too far, that he had over-emphasised the Son's sense of being abandoned, and that he had made it appear as if the Father had actually turned against his Son. He had made the cross, it was said, destroy the perpetual unity of the Father and Son, which is fundamental to Christian belief. But the critics were being unfair. For Moltmann made the crucial point that not even the cross could break the unity of the Trinity: Father and Son were united by their common will. Out of a shared love for humanity, they were willing together that the crucifixion should occur because they were one in heart and mind.

This oneness between Father and Son not only preserves the unity of the Trinity: it prevents us pushing the analogy between their relationship and human families too far. Often parent–child relationships cause pain because of a failure within the relationship. But on the cross there was no failure in the Father–Son relationship. The Son felt abandoned by the Father and the Father saw the Son as a rebel because of the breakdown of other relationships – between humanity and God.

There is an important difference, therefore, between the pain felt by the Father and the Son and similar hurts within ordinary families. We need to keep this in mind as we explore ways in

2. Jurgen Moltmann, *The Crucified God*, pp. 235–49.

which the Father and Son experienced some of the deepest pains of family life.

On the cross the Son felt the acute pain of being forsaken by his Father. There Jesus was, bearing extreme mental and physical torture. It was a time, surely, for the family to gather in support. But where was the heavenly Father? In the experience of Jesus he was nowhere it seems. For just before he died, Jesus cried out, 'My God! My God! Why have you forsaken me?' (Mark 15:34).

This was the only time that Jesus failed to address his Father as 'Abba', 'Daddy' almost. On all previous occasions, when praying to his Father, he had used this more intimate term because he felt so close to him. 'I am in the Father, and the Father is in me', Jesus had said (John 14:11). He had spent hours talking to him because he delighted to be in his company. Now he used the more distant title, 'God', because he felt abandoned by his Father.

Yet the Son also entrusted his life to his Father. 'Father, into your hands I commit my spirit' (Luke 23:46). He knew that he was totally dependent on his Father, but he also felt abandoned by him. He thus felt the most acute pain that a little child can ever bear – that sense of being forsaken by the person on whom he most depends. The baby who screams the house down because he fears mother has left him is expressing the agony of that pain. It may be significant that after describing how Jesus felt abandoned, Mark says that 'with a loud cry, Jesus breathed his last' (15:37).

To be abandoned by one's parents is perhaps the most painful form of rejection a child can experience. If a child grows up continually being criticised, no doubt she will feel rejected. But at least she knows her parents had some concern for her: they were concerned enough to criticise. Even if the criticism is motivated by a desire to use the child for the parents' own ends, at least the child is wanted enough to be used. The child who feels abandoned, however, cannot comfort herself with even that thought. Rejection frequently occurs within a relationship: to feel abandoned is to experience no relationship, which is the most painful thing of all.

The Father's experience at the crucifixion, on the other hand, was to see his Son as a rebel. For Jesus died as our representative. 'He himself bore our sins in his body on the tree' (1 Pet. 2:24). All our sins amount to one thing – rebellion against God.

FAMILY DELIVERANCE

In representing us, therefore, the Son took on values (our values) which were the exact opposite to what the Father stood for. So when parents feel aggrieved because their children have not turned out the way they hoped, when they feel devastated because their children have utterly abandoned the values they were brought up with, they experience something of what the heavenly Father must have felt when he looked at his rebellious Son.

There is a third dimension to this family crucifixion. The Son hung there as the family scapegoat. Now scapegoating occurs when family members collude together to allow it. Painful feelings which people within families cannot handle themselves are transferred unfairly on to their family's scapegoats – the sister, for example, who is madly jealous of her brother and so blames him for being jealous; or the father who diverts his fear of failure by denigrating his son. Scapegoating occurs when these feelings are not distributed round the family, but are dumped unceremoniously on one person. The collusion that makes this possible is one of the first things that family therapists look for.

Similar collusion occurred at the crucifixion. The Father did not intervene on his Son's behalf. He allowed us, the Son's brothers and sisters in his family, to put Jesus on the cross. He allowed Jesus to bear our sins – he gave permission for our sins to be offloaded on to his Son – so that we could be made sinless. Paul puts it more strongly, the Father 'did not spare his own Son, but gave him up for us all' (Rom. 8:32).

The Son joined the collusion by refusing to use the power at his disposal to stop it. He actively gave himself up for us (Eph. 5:2). Family therapists find that scapegoats invariably collude with the rest of the family, because they fear it would be more painful to bring the scapegoating to an end. Sometimes they are afraid the family will be destroyed. Perhaps the Son colluded because he knew that without the cross his family of women and men would be destroyed: he would have lost his brothers and sisters.

When therapists talk about collusion, they normally think of it as an unconscious process with pathological results. The crucifixion, by contrast, was knowingly willed by the Father and the Son, and had beneficial results. So there is not an exact parallel between what happened on the cross and the collusion which occurs within human families. However, some comparison can be made since on the part of Jesus' brothers and sisters the collusion was indeed unconscious. They were unaware that they were tieing into the Father's will. And in the short term the effect on God's family was extremely damaging. The Son's scream, 'My God! My God! Why have you forsaken me?', is a cry of anguish.

At the cross, then, Father and Son experienced some of the central hurts of family life. The Son felt not the caring love of his parent that the Old Testament calls for, but utterly abandoned by his Father. The Father experienced his Son not as someone who honoured him, but as a rebel – like so many of the Old Testament sons who rebelled. The result was rather like David's family (or Jacob's for that matter). The siblings turned on each other. This time it was not Amnon who was killed, but Jesus.

A healed family

The effect of the cross was to bring into existence the global family which human families were unable to create on their own. Those who believe are adopted into this family. God becomes their Father and Jesus their brother. Why did the Father and the Son have to bear the core pain of human families, rejection, in order to establish this family?

Part of the answer is that the means by which the family was created had to be consistent with its glorious nature. It is well-known how means can pervert their ends. The French Revolution had the goal of liberty, but the violence which brought about the revolution destroyed freedom. A mother may want to teach her child to be well behaved, but if she employs the wrong means – too much discipline for example – the child may eventually rebel and become even worse behaved. Means affect the ends. God chose means which would not frustrate his ends.

First, the Son did not use the power and authority he had at his disposal. He abandoned these so-called 'masculine' traits (which are by no means exclusive to men, nor always exercised by men) by adopting the more 'feminine' ones (so-called) of humbling himself to become human, and submitting to the cross.[3]

3. Angela West, 'A Faith for Feminists?', Jo Garcia and Sarah Maitland (eds.), *Walking on the Water*, pp. 66–90.

That is not to say that he completely rejected 'masculine' characteristics. Even now he is ruling over the world as its head, a very 'masculine' role (Col. 1:16ff).

Rather, he adopted 'feminine' traits in order to give up equality with God and become equal with men and women (Phil. 2:6ff). The Son was concerned about equality, which as we saw in chapter 7 was to be a characteristic of God's family. He hasn't forced us into submission by exercising a 'male' dominance which would leave us oppressed and take our freedom away. He preferred to win us over by coming alongside us, with a status equal to ours.

This equality was necessary if there was to be solidarity between the Son and us. Jesus had to become human to enter into our experience. It was because he was one of us, on the cross as our representative, that he could demonstrate the ultimate in solidarity – he could hang in place of us. This has made it possible for the Father and the Son to feel the pain of family. The Father could see his Son as a rebel, and the Son felt abandoned by his Father – the most acute form of rejection; he also felt rejected by the rest of the family. Sharing that pain has given them something in common with us.

Now the more you have in common with a person the closer you draw to them. A person going through divorce will feel more understood by a friend who has also separated than by someone who has no idea what it is like. One of the things that draws members of God's family together is having the same experiences of family failure as the Father and the Son, and knowing that they both understand. Thanks to the cross, we have been in the same boat together, and we can experience together the relief of being understood.

Solidarity was necessary if people were to be freed from the pain of rejection. For one reason why rejection hurts so much is that the rejected person feels unlovable. The child who is ignored by her parents may wonder, 'What's wrong with me that my parents should think I'm not worth paying attention to? What am I missing that would make them notice me?' Parents who feel rejected by their child may ask, 'What mistakes did we make? What was wrong with us that she should reject our values?' Rejection makes a person feel inadequate.

But the cross stands against that. It says that despite our failures we are not too inadequate for God. The Son endured the agony of being abandoned by his Father because he thought that we were worth loving. The Father experienced the anguish of seeing his Son as a rebel because he thought the same.

No emotional pain is as great as that experienced in families. Families, more than any other group, scar us for life. Indeed, often we are only wounded by other people because what they say or do triggers the unconscious memory of a deep family hurt. That the Father and Son *chose* to endure this family pain shows how valuable we are to them. However much we feel rejected by our parents or by our children, by our brothers or our sisters, we have not been rejected by God. (And he is the one who counts!) Knowing that is the first step to being freed from the pain of feeling not good enough.

In chapter 7 we saw that human families were to create a glorious family in which there would be equality, solidarity and liberty. We can see now that the Father and Son chose means appropriate to the ends, the way of equality and solidarity, to bring liberty to those who have been hurt by their families.

This freedom is not from outside oppression – from slavery, starvation and centralisation. It is from oppression inside, from the feeling that 'I'm not good enough', from that knock to the self-esteem which saps emotional energy, undermines self-confidence and prevents the person from relating positively to others at home.

Julie, a teenager, described the pain of never having lived up to her father's expectations, and how resentful she felt towards him. Then she described how she had discovered Jesus and learnt that she was accepted by God. As she understood that truth the pain of being rejected gradually became less, till she found that she could begin to forgive her father. The cross not only brings healing to individuals: it brings reconciliation to the family.

9

Family destination

A little girl was crying on the beach. Her two brothers were playing catch, and she felt left out. One of them threw the ball at the girl. She threw it back. Through her tears came a sandy smile. She was now part of the game. Thanks to the cross, believers have been brought into God's game. The Father and Son have extended their family to include those on the outside. We can have a sense of belonging which will make us smile again.[1]

The person who brings us into this family is the Holy Spirit, 'the Spirit of adoption'. It is he who brings the spirit of the family into our lives, by enabling the Father and the Son to 'make their home' with us; he makes it possible for us to speak to God as a Father (John 14:23; Rom. 8:14ff; Eph. 3:18). He also gives us the family likeness through his work of sanctification. God's family is Trinitarian, then, in that it is the Holy Spirit who bonds us to the Father and Son. He is just as important as the other two.

The Spirit is able to bring us into God's family because of what was accomplished on the cross. There the Father and the Son lifted from human families their failure fully to create God's family. What human families were unable to do on their own, God has now made possible. They can still contribute to God's family despite their mistakes, for mistakes are not fatal. However bad families may be, they can never thwart the building of God's family.

The time will come when all the tears of family life will be wiped away, when all the injustices will be forgotten, and we shall experience in wonder and joy 'the glorious freedom of the children of God' (Rom. 8:21). So instead of looking back

---

1. I'm grateful to the Revd James Jones for pointing me to this way of thinking about adoption into God's family.

and ruminating over past mistakes, we can look forward with eager anticipation.

We can experience, what's more, some of this future now. As the Spirit brings families closer to the Father and the Son and makes us more like them, and as he brings the spirit of God's family into our homes, we receive a foretaste of the family in heaven. Indeed, that has now become the main task of human families. They are to be a channel for the future. By the quality of their lives, they are to bring the future into the present.

But before seeing how that happens, we need briefly to look at the future. What is God's family like?

A global family

The New Testament teaches that Christians become members of a new community. The community already exists, but has yet to reach perfection in heaven. A variety of pictures are used to describe that community. 'Kingdom' and 'body' are two of the most common.

It might be thought that these metaphors warn against seeing God's community exclusively as a family, which has been our emphasis up to now. Could it be that the Bible's family language is simply another picture to help us understand something that is indescribable, and that we should hang this picture alongside the others but not give it pride of place?

The answer is almost certainly no. Family is the very essence of God's community. We know this first because Jesus implies that the nation of Israel, which originally was to have been the vehicle for creating God's community, should be seen as a family. It was to have been a community with a family character.

Jesus does this by identifying himself with Israel. He applies to himself Old Testament descriptions of Israel, such as that of the vine. 'I am the vine', Jesus said (John 15:5). In addition, he adopted the title 'Son of God', which had also been used to describe Israel (e.g. Exod. 4:22f), and made it the key to his identity (e.g. Matt. 11:27; John 5:25). His life was driven by the conviction that he was doing his Father's will (John 5:19). He spent hours in prayer to his Father.

The implication was clear. Because Jesus saw himself as

'Israel', as the expression of all that Israel should have been, and because Sonship was the key to Jesus' identity, so 'sonship' was the key to Israel's identity. Israel should have enjoyed the same family-type relationship to God as Jesus did. Israel was not merely the sum-total of Abraham's descendants: it was descended from the Father. It was his 'son', his family. It was more than God's special people, just as Jesus was more than God's special person. It was his family, like Jesus was his Son.

Secondly, Jesus makes it clear that the new Israel, the Church, should be seen as a family also. His mission was to set up God's Kingdom, but Jesus described that Kingdom in family rather than political terms. So he tells his followers to call God 'Father'. Nowhere are they commanded to address God as king. Believers have the status of 'sons' (which includes daughters) rather than of slaves or servants (John 8:35f; Luke 15:11ff).

Paul draws the obvious conclusion that if believers are 'sons' of one Father then they must also be 'brothers'. He describes them as such in almost every paragraph of his letters. If you look at his language, his favourite picture of the church is the family.[2] The term 'Kingdom' is used to highlight the *fact* that God rules. As to the nature of God's Kingdom: it is a royal family in which the Father reigns supreme.

Thirdly, the other terms that are used of God's community underline particular aspects of its family character. They do not contradict it. For example, the 'body' metaphor used by Paul highlights the closeness of family relationships. So when Paul, comparing the church to a body, says that if one part suffers every part suffers with it, what he is doing is emphasising the systemic closeness of God's family. We are all bound up with each other.

Someone may ask, 'But isn't all the Bible's language about God picture language anyway? How literally should we take these family terms?' This raises a highly technical question about the nature of religious language, which is too complicated to discuss here. Suffice to say that there are many experts who believe that the Bible's language about God does describe quite accurately what God is like. God is not so different to men and women that human language is unable to portray him at

2. Robert Banks, *Paul's Idea of Community*, p. 53.

all.[3] To speak of him as Father tells us that his community has essentially a family character.

It is also a community which will have a physical existence in the next life, as well as in this. Some people would deny this. They think that heaven is a spiritual, non-physical realm. But it is significant that God's intention was that Adam and Eve's descendants should spread over the world, pushing back – presumably – the boundaries of their idyllic garden as they did so. There is no obvious reason why beings who were made for a physical paradise at the beginning of history should be rewarded with a non-physical existence at the end of history.

The Bible suggests that Jesus came physically alive from the dead, and will return in a physical body to be united with his followers. His resurrection is presented as a foretaste of ours (e.g. 1 Cor. 15:1ff). We shall have physical bodies too. And physical bodies need a physical environment. That is why the New Testament describes heaven as a 'new earth' and 'new city'. Believers will inhabit something like a physical world, but it will be devoid of sin. As brothers and sisters with one Father, they will belong to a global family.

That will radically affect how we think about the application of 'Kingdom' ethics today. When we work for the Kingdom here on earth, we shall give priority to creating family-style relationships in society because that is the essence of the Kingdom. So we shall look at ways of making bureaucracies more 'homely', of strengthening local communities so that people feel they belong, of making sure that – where necessary – people receive in society the sort of care they should receive at home.

We may conclude that because means affect the ends, families should have a key role in countering the depersonalisation of modern society (though we must be careful not to exaggerate this). And this may require measures designed to reinforce family life. Advancing the Kingdom will be seen as advancing a family.

---

3. For a standard discussion of some of the issues, see I. T. Ramsey, *Religious Language*.

A Godly family

In February 1982 a brother and sister made headline news. They met for the first time after forty years of separation. Their family had been captured by the Nazis and sent to different concentration camps. They both survived, though neither knew where the other lived.

Years passed, and then thanks to another relative they were both united. Newspapers described the reunion. It seemed that in spite of years apart in two very different countries, brother and sister found that nothing could alter the fact that they belonged together in a very special way.[4]

In their book on the family, Ray Anderson and Dennis Guernsey quote research to show that brotherly and sisterly ties are the most lasting of human relationships. They outlive marriages. They precede children. They can be deeper than friendships because there is less need to pretend: the other person knows all about your past. You are accepted for who you are.[5]

Perhaps it is significant therefore that God's family is structured around two axes, the first of which is brotherly (and sisterly) relationships. Those who are adopted into the family become sisters and brothers of Jesus, and of each other. As such they will acquire a family likeness, which will resemble Jesus (Rom. 8:29). It is almost as if we shall become his identical twins, except there are millions of us. These relationships will last for ever, just as sisterly and brotherly bonds now tend to outlive other relationships. The enduring quality of sibling ties in this life reminds us of the family's eternal nature in the next.

Relatively speaking, the more important axis is Father and son. Sonship is *given* to members of God's family through the Holy Spirit. Our status does not therefore depend on us. It is as secure as the legal status of a child who has been adopted into a new family. Whatever the child does, however he feels, nothing can alter the fact that he belongs to that family.

The Spirit will write God's laws in these sons' hearts (cf. Jer. 31:33). This means that in heaven there will be no possibility of the sons disobeying their Father. God's laws will have been

4. Quoted by George Carey, *The Meeting of the Waters*. London 1985, p. 68.
5. Ray S. Anderson and Dennis B. Guernsey, *On Being Family: A Social Theology of the Family*. Grand Rapids, Eerdmans 1985, pp. 158–9.

permanently passed to the next generation, who will perpetually honour the Father. The Spirit will accomplish what human families failed fully to achieve. The Godly nature of the family will have been secured – for ever.

If parent–child and brotherly–sisterly relationships are the backbone of God's family, where does that leave marriage? Jesus promised that there will be no marrying in heaven (Mark 12:25). We do not know why that will be. Some people think that it is because there will be no child-raising. Marriage was originally given in the context of building a family that would inhabit the world. If the population in heaven is complete, there will be no need for more children – and so no need for marriage.

It is just as likely, however, that there will be no marrying because earthly marriages will find their counterpart in the richness of the heavenly community. All the joys of marriage – the intimacy, the acceptance, the belonging, the humour, the excitement of exploring new things together, learning from each other – presumably these and many more will be surpassed by the quality of relationships in the next life. These relationships will be as rewarding as marriage at its best. The fulfilment the individual is meant to find through one relationship in marriage will be found through a whole variety of relationships in heaven.

In heaven singleness will be the norm because community will be much richer. This means that from the standpoint of eternity, it is the exclusiveness of marriage – rather than singleness – which is the exception. So we should not despise singleness in this life. We should prize it highly, as a reminder of God's preferred status in the next. We should strive to build communities which have a touch of heaven about them, where some of the joys of marriage are reflected in the quality of their relationships, and where single people can feel part of a wider family.

One of the dangers in writing about the family is that single people can feel left out. That could certainly happen if it was thought that family revolves round marriage. But God's family is not structured on marriage. The most important bond is between parent and child. That was the first family relationship to exist in the garden. It existed between Adam and his Father, God, and when that went wrong marriage went wrong. The parent–child – 'Father'–'sonship' – relationship will be pivotal in the next paradise, too. We shall be united as brothers and sisters in obedience to the Father.

Far from single people being on the edge of family, therefore, from God's point of view they are central to it. Singleness will be universal in his family, and the key relationship will be between the Father and his children. What single person has never had a parent?

Creating a glorious family

God's family will bring out the best in people. Paul makes that clear when he likens the Church, God's family, to a bride who is presented to her husband radiantly beautiful without blemish. Because of what Jesus has done on the cross, he says, the Church will be made perfect like a bride (Eph. 5:25ff). It is God who will make us morally perfect. But presumably it is relationships within God's family that will refine us in other ways. They will be the means of bringing out hidden character traits and abilities.

It seems likely that these brotherly and sisterly relationships will be based on equality. This is despite the fact that the Bible uses predominantly masculine terms to describe members of that family – Father, Son(s) and brothers. This language might be thought to suggest a preference for masculine traits, which could imply male superiority in heaven.

Yet the Father is not exclusively masculine in character. The metaphor of mother is used to speak of God's pity (e.g. Ps. 22:9; Isa. 42:14). Deuteronomy 32:18 sees God as having a fatherly begetting role and a motherly giving-birth role. Godlikeness is expressed in both sexes (Gen. 1:27). God is a 'Motherly Father'.[6]

The Son (who reveals the Father) illustrated the maternal tenderness of God in his cry over Jerusalem (Matt. 23:37). He displayed the roles which we have been conditioned to regard as feminine of washing feet (John 13:1ff), making breakfast (John 21:12), teaching his male disciples to wait at table (Luke 9:16) and cuddling babies (Luke 18:15). He embodied the

---

6. Jurgen Moltmann, 'The Motherly Father. Is Trinitarian Patripassianism Replacing Theological Patriachalism?' in J.-B. Metz and E. Schillebeeckx (eds.), *God as Father*. New York 1981, pp. 51–6.

wisdom of God, which in the Old Testament is personified as 'she' (1 Cor. 1:30; Prov. 8:1).

In Colossians 1:15 Paul describes Jesus as the 'image' of the invisible God. Remembering what we said about God's image in Genesis 1:27 being reflected in the man and the woman as they related together, this may imply that Jesus combines 'masculine' and 'feminine' traits equally in himself. Certainly during his lifetime he seemed to display as many traits which are traditionally regarded as 'feminine' as he did 'masculine'. Not least, as we saw in the last chapter, he gave up his 'masculine' authority next to the Father in order to submit – a so-called 'feminine' trait – to the cross.

The Bible refers to God as 'he' to underline that he is a person. It avoids neutral language like 'it' because that would depersonalise God. Alternating 'he' and 'she' would depersonalise him too, for we never refer to a person as 'he' one day and 'she' the next.

But why does God choose to reveal himself as a 'he' and not 'she'? Perhaps in the Old Testament it was partly to reduce the likelihood of him being confused with the female deities of the surrounding Canaanite religion. Perhaps it was to accommodate the male chauvinism that has dominated history. He would be less likely to persuade a male-dominated world that he ruled over it if he presented himself as a woman.

What seems clear is that the language of God does not imply that he prefers traits which are stereotyped as 'masculine' because they are superior. Almost the reverse! Particularly as reflected in the life of Jesus, God seems to embrace the 'feminine' as readily as he does the 'masculine'. They have equal value in his eyes. This suggests that men and women will relate as people with equal value in heaven. (The term 'brothers' in the New Testament clearly includes sisters!)

Jesus told stories to show that equality will be one of the hallmarks of heaven. So in the parable of the vineyard, the labourers start work at different times of the day. But they all get the same pay regardless of when they started (Matt. 20:1ff) – they are not covered by union rates! Jesus is making the point that salvation, the gift of a place in his family, is given equally to any who receive it. 'The last will be first, and the first will be last' (v. 16). God has no favourites. That is the basis of equality.

It may be significant that in Jesus' story about the wedding feast, a picture of heaven, the poor get the same meal as the rich would have done if they had not declined the invitation (Luke 14:15ff). The benefits of the Kingdom are to be equally distributed. That is in line with what God had intended for Israel, where land was supposed to have been parcelled into family holdings of roughly equal size. There is no obvious reason why God should have been concerned for equality in his family then, but not in the future.

This should help us to understand what Jesus said about some people having larger rewards in heaven than others (Matt. 25:14ff). It is not certain what these rewards refer to. They may be different degrees of responsibility – some will have more than others. If that is the case, what is clear is that this responsibility will not be authoritarian. People will not lord it over others; they will serve them by putting their interests first. There will be liberty from oppression (Mark 10:42ff).

God's family will be a glorious family because it will bring out the best in people through relationships of equality. All our blemishes will be taken away. Then as we relate to each other, is it too much to imagine that our potential will be drawn out first by one person and then by another? Perhaps one person will stimulate an interest in music, someone else in art. One person may teach us one thing, another something different. And so we shall continue perhaps, for all eternity, releasing in each other more and more of our potential within a community where everyone is equal.

What a contrast with the unfair treatment many have experienced in human families – the second child for example, who seethes because the eldest by being first got hold of things, while the youngest by being last got away with things. She carries that resentment into adulthood, where it still creates tension at home.

The promise of God's family is that when it reaches home in all its glory, these injustices will be put right. Those who were treated unequally in their families will see the fairness to which they are entitled. Those who are made to feel incomplete by their parents, who think there must be something missing – something wrong – with them for their parents to find them so unlovable, will find themselves completed in heaven. All the good that was crushed out of them at home will be released inside their 'Father's house'. Human families are not the last word. There is hope for those who despair.

That is why the cross is such good news. We have seen how human families were supposed to create an international family that would remain loyal to God in relationships of equality, solidarity and liberty. We have seen how they made no more than the most modest of starts. We have seen how through the cross, by experiencing the acute hurts of family life, the Father and the Son resurrected that family from the death it would otherwise have suffered.

In this chapter we have seen how this family will be established as a global family – a community with a family character, set in a physical environment akin to a new earth. We have seen how it will remain a godly family because the law will have been written in its children's hearts, and how it will be a glorious family because the potential of its members will be drawn out through relationships of equality. God will do what human families have been unable to complete.

That brings hope to the lonely: they will have the joy of belonging. It brings hope to those outside families: they will not feel excluded because everyone will be single. It brings hope to those who have been unfairly treated at home: justice will be restored and hurts made whole. The next three chapters will show that this hope is not just for the future: it is also for the present. It can make a difference now.

PART FOUR
Enthused families

10

Extended out

An artist who is to begin painting will normally have some idea of what the finished picture will be like. He may not see the end result clearly, but he will have something in mind to work toward. As he paints, his mental picture of the completed work will come increasingly into focus, and this may spur him on. It may encourage him to change what is on the canvas, so that it conforms more closely to the ideal he is trying to create.

The power of the future

In recent years a number of theologians have emphasised the power of God's future to rouse us to change the present, rather as a vision of what the canvas could become challenges the artist to transform it. In *Theology of Hope*, for example, Jurgen Moltmann argued that God reveals himself in Scripture through his promises. These promises point to a future which is radically different to the present. Men and women experience God as they seek to change the present so that it conforms more closely to the future God will prepare for them.

We have seen how the Old Testament contains insights which, if taken to heart, would have challenged Israelite families to work toward the creation of an expanding nation, with a family character and with relationships of equality, solidarity and liberty that reflected God's glory. This goal of family life, the future, would have influenced the behaviour of Israelite families in the present.

We have also seen how the Father and Son have rescued their family of women and men from human failure, and how followers of Christ have been adopted into this family and are members of it. That means they can describe it as 'my family'. They can identify with it and feel part of it. What this family will be like, therefore, should mean a lot to them. For just as children will be influenced by the values of their family, so Christians should be influenced by the values of God's family, which will reach perfection in heaven. They should own them, because as members of God's family its values belong to them. These values should affect what they do in the here and now.

Moreover, Scripture models these values for us. It provides examples of these values being worked out in practice. There is a world of difference between being told what to do and being shown how to do it. The Old Testament emphasis is on instruction – on what families should do to create God's family. The New Testament adds a new dimension. It presents models of how people will behave in God's family when all its shortcomings have been removed. These models show human families how they should live today. They enable the future to confront the present with increased power.

In this and the next two chapters we shall see how these models challenge family behaviour in the modern world.

Starting a family

The first example is how the future makes marriage an option. Society tends to see marriage as the norm for most people at some stage. Despite the pain of their first marriage, some seventy per cent of American divorcees are expected to remarry. Marriage is regarded as automatic. Because it is such a natural step, it is not seen as a calling, a way of life to be deliberately chosen. Marriage is something everybody does.

We saw in the last chapter how God's family is organised on very different lines. The basic relationships are between the Father and his children, and between the Son and his sisters and brothers. There will be no marrying in heaven. People will find ultimate satisfaction as they relate to each other as single persons. In eternity the absurd person will not be singular, but the one who expects to be married.

Since this future is meant to challenge the present, it is no surprise to find Jesus making singleness an option for the here and now. He stood against the Jewish expectation that everyone should marry by living a life of singleness himself. This provides a model of the perfected life we shall one day enjoy. The New Testament describes Jesus' resurrection as the 'first-fruits', an anticipation, of ours (1 Cor. 15:20). The future resurrection of believers has been brought forward and modelled for us. In a similar way the singleness of Jesus brings forward and models our single status in heaven.

It shows in particular how the future state of singleness confronts expectations in the present. Jesus taught that his example of singleness was not just for himself, but was an option for his followers: some will stay single for the sake of the Kingdom (Matt. 19:12). Paul develops the point by arguing that singleness frees people from the concerns of this world so that they can commit themselves to making this life more like the next (1 Cor. 7:32ff). Jesus, then, provides a model which is meant to spur us to see singleness as a calling.

New Testament teaching on this subject, specially Paul's, has sometimes been thought to exalt singleness at the expense of marriage. But that is not so. If singleness is the norm from the standpoint of eternity, if it is worth remaining unmarried so that we can be single-minded about God's family, if in fact singleness is a calling, then marriage must be treated as a calling also, and valued as such.

It must not be seen as natural, something to be automatically entered into because everyone else is doing so. Marriage must be viewed as an explicit vocation. Individuals will ask, 'How does God want me to contribute to his family – by staying single or getting married?' They will consider whether they have the gifts for singleness (the gift of sexual abstinence for example), or the gifts for marriage (commitment, fidelity and so on). In particular they will ask whether they have been given the vision to help build God's family by creating a new biological family.

Entering marriage because one has been called to a vision of what it can achieve makes it more important. It makes it a specific calling, and the summons to a special task is always more significant than life's daily routine. So there is a paradox: by modelling the future, Jesus not only raised the status of singleness – he enhanced the value of marriage.

This has implications for how people are prepared for marriage. The aim will be to strengthen the couple's sense of mission to the world. They will be encouraged to test their vocation against the goal of family life, which is to help create God's family. They will be challenged to consider how far they both subscribe to that goal, whether they have weighed up the sacrifices involved, whether they have the gifts to achieve the goal, and how they will set about the task. This will be so embedded in the church's life that even before the couple are engaged they will be making decisions in the light of God's future.

Extending the family

Sarah was a single mother with two children. Outside her house one day she found a thirteen-year-old girl. A few questions elicited the fact that Amie had been abandoned by her parents, looked after by an aunt and uncle, and had now been abandoned by them. She had spent the past few nights in Sarah's garden shed. Looking at this 'dishevelled scrap', Sarah decided that she had no option but to take her in. God's family challenges the modern nuclear family to open its door to outsiders like Amie, and to develop 'fuzzy boundaries'.

One of the startling features of the family in heaven is its size. It will embrace all the followers of Jesus. This size is hinted at in Jesus' promise. 'In my Father's house are many rooms. . . I am going there to prepare a place for you' (John 14:2). He seems to have had in mind a picture similar to that in the Jewish book, *Book of the Secrets of Enoch*, which likens heaven to a vast palace with many rooms, one for each person.

In heaven all the boundaries between human families will be dissolved. There will be one global family inheriting a new earth. This provides a model which challenges the modern tendency to narrow the family down to a 'privatised' nuclear unit.

What this challenge may mean in practice was illustrated by the first Christians, who made virtually no distinction between the family household and the 'household of God'. Believers ate together, worshipped in their homes, showed hospitality to one another and shared their possessions. The church grew as key families opened their homes to outsiders. The house of Aquila and Priscilla, for example, became the embryonic centre of the church at Ephesus.

The home-based nature of the early church helped to give it a family feel. Members called each other 'brothers'. This was particularly important for those converts, specially Jewish ones, who had been cut off by their families because of their conversion. They found in their new family belonging and acceptance which compensated for the loss of their old families. Thanks to the openness of these early Christian homes, something of the extended nature of God's family had become a reality in their lives.

Modern families can bring the future into the present in a similar way by drawing in outsiders. Often these outsiders will be members of one's own extended family. In Britain 2.75 million people live on their own; one million do not see a friend, neighbour or relative even once a week.[1]

Caring for one's relatives by identifying those who have been forgotten, by phoning and visiting more often, by using anniversaries to bring the wider family together and by encouraging the family as a whole to provide financial support, perhaps, to an aging aunt who needs it, can be the first step in opening one's family to other people.

Another would be to include people outside the family, like Sarah wanted to do. When Sarah decided to take Amie in, as a single mother she was faced with the problem of having to cope on her own. She already had two children, and she knew that she could not look after a third.

She sought help from others in the church, who had recently become aware of the need to support single parents. They began to talk it through. But it was too late. A social worker had been called in, and he happened to mention, in earshot of Amie, that she might have to be taken into care. Amie was off before dawn – and never seen again.

Having missed one opportunity, the church resolved to be ready for the next. They decided that, with their families' agreement, men in the church should provide fathering roles to children in one-parent homes – playing with them, taking them out and so on. Families could then support existing mothers in need, and be ready to support outsiders like Amie. When families support each other like that, and when they draw outsiders into their lives, they begin to make the global family of the future a reality now.

---

1. Michael Schluter, 'Bringing the Extended Family Back to Life' in Richard Whitfield (ed.), *Families Matter. Towards a Programme of Action*. Marshall Pickering, Basingstoke 1987, pp. 208–16.

A family for families

If families share their lives with other people, they risk being so involved with outsiders that their members become exhausted and emotionally drained; they can be denied the privacy they need. Equally, when families turn in on themselves, they cut themselves off from important sources of outside support. A balance must be struck, and it will differ from home to home.

Families which identify with the extended model of God's family will begin to create a community in which they themselves are blessed. By supporting others, they will find that support is available to them. As families mix together, parents will be in a position to learn from each other. A mother who never learnt how to discipline from her own parents may see what to do from a friend. A father whose parents never played with him may discover how to play with his own children by watching other families.

Not least, families will receive emotional support from each other. Mothers will be less likely to feel isolated and alone. Marriages will be under less stress. Jack Dominian has described the potential of marriage to heal hurts from childhood. Since it is as intimate a relationship as between mother and child, marriage has the power to reverse the mistakes that were made in that first relationship. The rejected child can be emotionally healed as she experiences, year after year, acceptance by her spouse.[2]

But what happens if both parents have experienced such rejection that they are unable to accept each other sufficiently for the healing to occur? The couple will then need affirmation and acceptance from outside the marriage. This will come as they contribute to the life of the church and feel appreciated within it. As they are built up by their friends, the partners will feel stronger inside. Their capacity to love each other will grow. The marriage will be strengthened by being rooted in community. That is why God's family is for families. As families seek to make it a present reality, the quality of their own lives will be increased.

Here, then, are two models from the future which are important for families today. Jesus provides a model of the single

---

2. Jack Dominian, *Marriage, Faith and Love*, pp. 58–67.

status which will be ours in heaven. In so doing he made singleness an option, which means that marriage is a choice! Both in fact are vocations, and we must prayerfully decide to which we are called.

God's family will be an extended family – that's the second model, and just as New Testament families tried to make that a reality in their lives, we are to do the same. We are to support other families and open our homes. That will help to create a community which contains just a taste of heaven, and which will provide support for our own families. The end of the family is the end of family distinctions.

11

Handed on

Chris, a fourteen-year-old, was typical of countless teenagers in wanting to take control of her life, but finding that her parents would not let go. Her parents kept listening to her phone calls – the phone was in the dining room. Occasionally her father would cut off a call if it was from one of her boyfriends. A whole series of niggles showed that her parents were frightened of losing their daughter's love.

They had few friends and not much of a social life. So they received little affirmation from outside the family, which meant that they were particularly dependent on their four children to accept and value them. Chris was the eldest. Instead of spending time with the family, she wanted to be with her friends. Rather than accepting her parents' views, she wanted to make up her own mind. Her parents saw this as a threat. They saw it as the withdrawal of the love they desperately craved.

The frustrations Chris faced are experienced in homes time and again. What model of parent–child relationships does God's family provide?

The Father–Son relationship

The New Testament presents a model which is summed up in two verses. In Matthew 28:18 Jesus told his disciples, 'All authority in heaven and on earth has been given to me.' The Father has delegated to the Son the task of bringing to completion the Kingdom of God. Jesus has ushered in the Kingdom, but it has not yet been fully established. Though the authority was delegated in the past, therefore, there is also a future dimension. Authority *has been* given in order that God's Kingdom *will be* established. The delegation will continue into the future.

In 1 Corinthians 15:24 Paul promises that at the end of history Jesus will hand the Kingdom back to the Father. In so doing the Son recognises that the authority which he has received is not his own. He honours his Father by undertaking a task that is close to the Father's heart and presenting him with the completed work. Again there is a future dimension. The model comes from the future to challenge us in the present. What precisely does it involve?

Parenting

The Old Testament instructed parents to pass on knowledge of God to their children so that the next generation would know how to build God's family. A similar idea is involved in the delegation of authority over the Kingdom to the Son. The Father has passed on to the Son the task of establishing the Kingdom, which we have seen has a family character. The Son establishes this family by creating men and women, by overseeing human history and in particular by dying on the cross (Col. 1:15ff).

Just as parents in the Old Testament were to pass on knowledge of God in the context of a loving relationship with their children, so the Father hands over the Kingdom to the Son in the same kind of relationship, 'the Father loves the Son. . .' (John 5:20). This love involves the provision of security. 'Father, into your hands I commit my spirit', Jesus cried from the cross (Luke 23:46). He trusted his Father to look after him.

The love also involves praise and recognition. The Father has rewarded the Son for his obedience on earth by giving him the highest place in heaven next to himself, he has commanded the angels to worship him and he has praised him for his achievements (Phil. 2:9ff; Heb. 1:3ff). The love involves, too, the giving of responsibility – the Son is responsible for the Kingdom.

Research suggests that for children to develop healthily they need love and security, praise and recognition, responsibility and new experiences. This is the basis of Mia Kellmer Pringle's book, *The Needs of Children*.[1] The Father models these parental qualities in the way that he loves the Son.

The Old Testament implies that parental love requires communication. Again, Father and Son provide an example. The

1. M. K. Pringle, *The Needs of Children*. Hutchinson 1980.

Father speaks to the Son, who listens to what is said. On earth Jesus spent hours in prayer to his Father, and he still speaks to him on our behalf (Heb. 7:25); the Father listens. Their communication is emotionally honest. The Son 'offered up prayers and petitions with loud cries and tears. . .' (Heb. 5:7). The Father and Son's communication therefore is two-way, it entails listening, it is frequent and feelings are expressed. More than just words are exchanged:

> 'I only said "if"!' poor Alice pleaded in a piteous tone.
> The two Queens looked at each other, and the Red Queen remarked, with a little shudder, 'She *says* she only said "if". . .'
> 'But she said a great deal more than that!' the White Queen moaned, wringing her hands. 'Oh, ever so much more than that!'[2]

It is in the context of love that the Father teaches the Son. 'I do nothing on my own but speak just what the Father has taught me', Jesus said (John 8:28). 'My teaching is not my own. It comes from him who sent me' (John 7:16). Just as knowledge of God in ancient Israel was to be passed from one generation to the next, so the Son learns about the Father and passes that on to his disciples. At the end of his life Jesus could tell his Father that he has given his disciples 'the words you gave me and they accepted them' (John 17:8).

Since the Son was made 'like his brothers in every way' and the Father 'punishes everyone he accepts as a son' (Heb. 2:17; 12:6), one might expect the Son to experience his Father's discipline. In a sense he did so as he hung on the cross, a rebel in our place, bearing the punishment that should have been ours (2 Cor. 5:21; Gal. 3:13). Whereas the Israelite law taught parenting, the Father models it.

Separation

The Old Testament includes the insight that children must separate from parents and choose the faith for themselves. Again, the Father and Son model this for us. The Father has released his Son by delegating all authority to him. 'In putting everything under him, God left nothing that is not subject to him' (Heb. 2:8). The release is total.

2. Lewis Carroll, *Through the Looking Glass*. London 1971, p. 170.

Philippians 2:6ff suggests the idea of the Son choosing to separate from the Father. It was the Son 'who did not consider equality with God something to be grasped'. It was the Son 'who made himself nothing'. It was the Son who chose to humble himself. It was the Son, therefore, who decided to leave his place in heaven, where he was right beside the Father, and come to earth.

Since he started his human life in Mary's womb where he knew nothing, the Son had to leave all his knowledge behind. That meant that as he grew up he had to learn about his Father all over again. There's a sense in which he had to discover the faith for himself. It was because he chose to own the faith that he became of one mind with the Father, and it was this that preserved their unity despite the cross.

Honouring

Handing back the Kingdom contains the idea that the Son will have completed successfully the task given to him by the Father. Having learned obedience by what he suffered on earth (Heb. 5:8), the Son continues in obedience so that he can accomplish his Father's will.

But just as in the Old Testament honouring means more than obedience (it also means respect), so handing back the Kingdom implies that the Son does more than what his Father tells him: he respects his Father. He offers back to him what he has done, like an adult child might offer back his home by inviting an aging parent to live with him.

So Jesus doesn't do what the younger son did in the story of the Prodigal Son. In the parable the son asks for half the father's property. The moment he's got it, he takes off to a foreign country, spends it all and then returns home empty handed. The father gets nothing back from his son except a financial disaster and the son's recognition that he has made a mess of his life. The case of *the* Son is entirely different. The Father receives back from his Son all that he gave to him and countless more. He receives the venture delegated to his Son, successfully completed.

Parents and children among the first Christians

Jesus instructed his followers to be perfect as their heavenly Father is perfect (Matt. 5:48). Following that example, Paul told the Ephesian church to 'be imitators of God' (Eph. 5:1). It is clear that New Testament Christians saw God as a model. It seems, too, that they realised this model might challenge family relationships. Paul sees Christ's relationship to the church as a pattern for marriage (Eph. 5:22ff). He speaks of the Father from whom the whole family on earth derives its name (Eph. 3:14f). God's fatherhood is the source of all conceivable fatherhood. It is the model from which true parenting derives.

Parenting

When Paul wrote about the duty of parents, therefore, it is not surprising to find echoes of the Father's example. Paul would have been familiar with Old Testament passages like Hosea 11:1, where God's treatment of Israel is likened to a father's treatment of his child. But it is not inconceivable that he also had in mind the Father's parenting of the Son, which was in stark contrast to the treatment of children in many Roman homes. A Roman father could sell his children as slaves, he could make them work in his fields even in chains, and he could punish them unjustly. He was bound by few laws, for within the home he made the laws.

A callous cruelty prevailed in the Roman Empire. It was not unknown for unwanted babies to be abandoned, for weak and deformed ones to be killed, and for healthy children to be regarded as a partial nuisance because they inhibited sexual promiscuity and complicated divorce. It was against this background that Paul urged fathers (and the term included mothers) not to 'exasperate' their children (Eph. 6:4). This has the sense of not goading their children to resentment. Parental authority is to be exercised with restraint.

In particular, it is to be accompanied by love. When Paul in this verse tells parents to bring their children up, he uses a word which literally means to 'nourish' or 'feed'. It has the sense of building up, of strengthening a person. Calvin translated it, 'Let them be fondly cherished . . . deal gently with them.' 'Here is an understanding, centuries before modern psychology emphasised the vital importance of the earliest years of life, that children are fragile creatures needing the tenderness and security of love.'[3]

Parents are to bring children up in the 'instruction of the Lord', Ephesians 6:4 continues. This refers mainly to verbal education and includes teaching about the heavenly Father. Children are also to be trained by discipline, which is the literal meaning of the word in this verse translated sometimes as just 'training'. It is the same word as that used in Hebrews 12:7ff of the Father who disciplines his children.

Parents, then, were not to treat their children callously without love. Nor were they to impose their own values, for they were under God's authority and they were to teach their children what God required. Nor were they to discipline arbitrarily. Discipline was to reinforce what they taught and was to occur within a relationship of love. Christian parenting was to display the same characteristics as the Father's parenting of the Son.

Separating

Just as the Son separated from the Father by receiving authority from him, by choosing to leave heaven and by owning the faith for himself, so New Testament Christians were expected to separate from their parents. Jesus taught that loyalty to him was to have precedence over allegiance to one's parents (Luke 9:59ff). His followers were to break away from the culture of their sinful homes so that they could identify totally with God's family. An example was set by the disciples who gave up everything to follow Jesus.

Particularly for Jewish families, that could be costly. Children were expected to be totally loyal to their parents' faith. Jewish converts risked being disowned by their parents, expelled from the synagogue (which was a centre of their lives) and cut off by their friends. Jesus was being eminently realistic, therefore, when he warned that his ministry would lead to division within families (Luke 12:51ff).

There are hints that children of believing parents were expected not simply to copy their parents' faith, but to make it their own. In some of his letters Paul addressed children as well as adults (e.g. Eph. 6:1; Col. 3:20), which implies that

3. John Stott, *God's New Society. The Message of Ephesians*. IVP, London 1979, p. 247.

parents were not to be children's only source of instruction. Children were to learn from what was being taught to the congregation as a whole. As they grew into young men and women, they were to be trained in groups by others in the church (Titus 2:3ff). They were to have the chance to check out what they were learning at home and reach their own conclusions.

Honouring

As the Son honours his Father, children in the early church were expected to honour their parents. Paul taught, 'Children, obey your parents. . .' (Eph. 6:1). He was addressing younger children for whom obedience was appropriate, but he adds the significant qualification 'in the Lord. . .'. Obeying parents was not to have priority over following God. As the child grew up, his obedience was to be qualified by the need to be primarily loyal to the Lord.

Paul goes on to quote the fifth commandment, 'Honour your father and mother', and then he adds a promise which is a conflation of Exodus 20:12 and Deuteronomy 5:16, 'that it may go well with you and that you may enjoy long life on the earth.' In the Old Testament context the promise was concerned with material prosperity and long life for God's community. Paul's reference to 'on the earth' probably contains a similar idea. Social stability will be the mark of any community in which children honour their parents. If children have not learnt obedience at home, they will find it more difficult to accept authority outside the home.

Adult children were expected not to obey their parents so much as to respect them. They were to care for them (and their parents' parents) as they grew old, 'so repaying their parents and grandparents' (1 Tim. 5:4). The idea of repayment contains the thought of handing back to your parents something of what they have given to you. It is similar to the model of the Son handing back the Kingdom to the Father.

So it was that the Father–Son relationship was to be echoed in the early church. It embraced values which challenged the cultural norms of the first Christians, and which were reflected in the household codes of the New Testament (see also, for example, Col. 3:20f). How does it challenge families today?

Parents and children today

A challenge to parents

On the one hand it challenges the dominant father of Victorian novels who was emotionally distant from his children and used authority for his own ends. The modelling of love, including communication, by the Father amplifies Old Testament teaching on the subject. It provides an example of intimacy between father and child. Love insists that parents put the child's interests before their own, and this acts as a break on their authority. So too does the giving of steadily more responsibility to the child as she grows up. The Father provides an example of a parent releasing his son.

Using discipline in a relationship of love and taught values shows how discipline need not be reduced to appropriate punishment schemes, or to techniques of 'behaviour reinforcement' which penalise undesirable behaviour. When discipline is taken out of its proper context, a loving relationship in which morality is valued, it becomes a technique. Like training an animal, it becomes a means of controlling a child so that she pleases her parents. The child will grow up to resent her parents for being so manipulative.

Equally, the Father's model of parenting challenges the opposite, child rights approach to raising children. This says that the child has the right to do what she likes so long as she does not hurt others. She will learn best, and express her potential most fully, by doing and discovering what she wants. Love, so-called, is elevated to the point where teaching values is almost ignored.

Yet taught values, backed by discipline, enable children to know where they stand. Children like achieving, learning and being stretched, and they feel safe if they know what they can do and what they can't. If the boundaries are firm, a child will know how far he can go before he oversteps the mark. But if they are unclear and his parents are inconsistent, so that they shout at him one moment but when he does it again they scarcely respond, the child will become anxious. He may become over-cautious, worried how his parents will react, or even more of a rebel as he keeps on pushing at the boundary to see how far he can go.

That parenting is modelled by the Father, singular, may have some significance. It shows one person combining in himself the so-called motherly trait of love, and the so-called fatherly quality of discipline. Perhaps it is a reminder that these characteristics do not belong exclusively to particular genders. 'Motherly' and 'fatherly' roles can be carried out by either sex. Mothers frequently discipline and fathers often show love. Children in one-parent homes will not necessarily be deprived of the role model of the missing parent, though it is always difficult in practice for one parent to do the job of two.

A challenge to children

The Son models how children should honour their parents. He learns from the Father how he should build God's Kingdom, and then he hands back to his Father the finished project. Children should learn from their parents how to build God's Kingdom, and they should hand back to their parents – as it were – their achievements in taking forward the Kingdom.

In Christian families, an adult child does this when she shows her parents explicitly how what she learnt at home is helping her to achieve their spiritual goals. She might show them, for example, how she is teaching her children to pray like they taught her as a child. She might mention how the qualities of honesty and fairness, which she learnt at home, have influenced what she does at work. In talking about her life, occasionally she will highlight how her parents made it possible for her to accomplish what she did.

Where the parents are not believers, it will still be possible for the child to acknowledge what he has received from them – a stable home perhaps, encouragement to carry on with a musical instrument, the financial help to go to college, or whatever. All these are gifts which may enable the child to advance the Kingdom in some way. He can show that he appreciates his parents for these gifts, without labouring the spiritual context in which the gifts are now viewed.

The 'handing back' model is really a model for handing on, from one generation to the next. It makes explicit what is merely implied in the Old Testament – that in respecting one's parents, one should take from them only what will help to advance the cause of God's family. Honouring is not morally neutral.

It also assumes, as in the Old Testament, that children have forgiven their parents. It is hard to be positive toward our parents if we are resentful about their mistakes. Resentment focuses attention away from the good within parents. It ruminates on their failures. To acknowledge their qualities, resentment must be overcome through forgiveness. Handing back the Kingdom challenges us to forgive our parents.

If we do this and acknowledge what we have received from them, our parents will feel affirmed. We shall give back to them some of the love we have received from them, and that will help them to continue to affirm us in return. Mutual affirmation will bridge the gap between generations and draw families together. Forgiving our parents will begin to heal the hurts we suffered from them, while affirming our parents will start to heal hurts they experienced from us.

Family therapist and best-selling author, Robin Skynner, has described a case slightly reminiscent of Chris's parents at the beginning of the chapter.

> In one of the first cases I treated as a family, the problem *appeared* to be the daughter. . . She had upset the parents from the age of two up to the age of fourteen – which is when she was sent to me – and the mother had actually spent many spells in mental hospitals and made several suicide attempts. After four sessions of family therapy, the mother began to be able to acknowledge her deep craving for love and affection. As this happened, the daughter stopped her misbehaviour and became the one who gave the mother the love she'd never had. The mother didn't need to go to hospital again.[4]

Families can be centres of healing and reconciliation if we allow the model of the Father–Son relationship to make a difference today.

---

4. Robin Skynner/John Cleese, *Families and How to Survive Them*, pp. 126–7.

12

Reflected back

Sheila MacLeod, writing about her anorexia, has described how she was brought up by parents neither of whom was willing to assume leadership. Her two sisters wore clothes and make-up designed solely to acquire boyfriends.

> Meetings were held in secret – the boy with the bus fare or the motor-bike waiting at the end of the lane – and elaborate lies told as a cover-up until my parents got wise to what was going on.
> They argued endlessly about it. 'You tell her.' 'No, you tell her.' 'You're her mother.' 'You're the one who's getting so worked up about it.' My father would rage and storm, not so much at my mother as to her, and against Helen and Pat in their absence, but in the end neither of them would say anything to either of my sisters.

Sheila's figure of suspicion pointed to parents who succeeded in an extraordinary combination of inaction and intolerance. An atmosphere of tension and suppressed resentment prevailed.

Perhaps the greatest gift that parents can give to their children is themselves. As they spend time with each other and as they learn to express their feelings accurately, to be patient and to forgive, parents will discover how to love and affirm one another. They will feel more able to love their children, and they will provide better models for their children to copy.

This requires the parents to act as a team, sharing the responsibilities and supporting each other, rather than abdicating authority – as in Sheila's home – and blaming one another. But how can they build this team? In chapter 11 we saw how God's global family challenges nuclear families to open their doors to people outside the home. The last chapter showed how parent–child relationships are challenged by the Father–Son relationship within that family. In this chapter we shall look first at the challenge posed to marriage by God's glorious family.

The challenge to equality

In Ephesians 5:22ff Paul, in his fullest statement on marriage, presents Christ's relationship to the Church as a model for marriage. Just as Christ died for the Church to make her perfect, husbands are to give themselves to their wives and bring out the best in them. The wife is to respond by submitting to her husband. We have made the point that when the Son came to earth he gave up what is stereotyped as a 'masculine' position of authority next to the Father, and adopted the so-called 'feminine' quality of submission to the cross. Here Paul is making a related point: submission is appropriate for both men and women.

As with the Father–Son relationship, the model described by Paul has a backward and forward dimension. It looks back to what Jesus did on the cross. The future judgement that would have been ours has been brought into the past and borne by Jesus. But it looks forward to what the cross achieves, which is the eventual perfection of God's family. So as before, this is a model which will only be completed in the future. It is this finished, future relationship which challenges the present.

Paul has frequently been thought to advocate male headship within marriage exercised in a considerate way. But a close look at Ephesians 5:22ff shows that Paul is really talking about mutual submission in marriage. He starts, in verses 22–4, by addressing wives. They are to submit to their husbands. Now this has the idea of self-giving, of surrender to the other person's interests. It does not mean obedience. If Paul had wanted to talk about obedience he would have used the verb 'obey', as he does when speaking of children and slaves in chapter 6.

The reason wives are to submit to their husbands is given in verse 23 – because the husband is the head of the wife. What exactly does this mean? In the Greek 'head' can have a variety of meanings. It can mean authority ('head of the home'); it can mean origin or beginning (the head of a procession); and it can mean completion (when you bring a disagreement to a head you try to resolve it, or bring it to completion).

There are good reasons for thinking that Paul is using 'head' in this third sense of completion. First, in 4:15 Paul has just used 'head' in talking about the church as a body. Clearly in that verse Christ is head in the sense of completion, for – Paul says – he enables the church, the body, to grow into maturity. When a person is mature, their natural development is complete. And that is what Christ, as its head, helps the church to become – complete. Having in chapter 4 used 'head' in the sense of completion, one might expect Paul to give it the same meaning a few paragraphs later when, talking about marriage, he again thinks of the church as a body. 'For the husband is head of the wife as Christ is head of the church, his body. . .' (v. 23).

Secondly, at a grammatical level this passage about marriage (from verse 22 on) is linked inseparably to verse 21. One verb, 'submit', governs both verses 21 and 22. Paul states a general principle in verse 21, 'Submit to one another out of reverence for Christ.' He then applies that principle to marriage. Now if Christians are to submit to one another as a matter of course, it cannot only be the wife who is to submit: the husband must do so too. That means that Paul cannot be talking about headship in terms of the husband's authority. The immediate context rules it out. Verse 21, with its direct link to what follows, is all about mutual submission.

Thirdly, verse 23 itself indicates that Paul is talking about headship in terms of completion. For Paul says that 'the husband is the head of the wife as Christ is the head of the Church, his body, *of which he is the Saviour.*' What does the work of the Saviour involve? Paul explains in verse 26ff. Jesus saves the Church by making her spotless, without blemish. He brings the Church to completion by making her perfect.

The general context, the immediate context and the verse itself all point in the same direction. Wives are to submit not because their husbands are in authority, but because the husband seeks to complete his wife by bringing out the best in her. He is giving himself to her in her interests. The wife should submit because the husband should have her interests at heart.

This might have encouraged wives to think that they were the takers in a relationship where husbands did the giving. So Paul continues, 'But' – significantly, the word which opens verse 24 is a strong one – this is no excuse for the wife to relax in her duties. She should reciprocate. She should submit to her husband like the Church submits to Christ (v. 24).

Having talked about wives, in verse 25 Paul turns to the role of husbands. They are to love their wives just as Christ loved the Church. Their love is to be like Christ's. But what is the nature of Christ's love? The rest of the verse explains – 'who gave himself up for the church'. The husband's love is to be sacrificial. It is to be self-giving in the interests of his wife, which of course is the basic meaning of submission. When I submit to someone I put their interests first: when I make a sacrifice for a person, again I put their interests first. There is no essential difference between love and submission. Husbands and wives are to submit to one another, just as all Christians should submit to each other. The relationship is one of equality, in which submission is mutual.

If that is what Paul meant, then why did he not make it clearer by using the word submission with reference to husbands, and by finding an alternative to the ambiguous term 'head'? Perhaps the answer is that Paul knew how radically his teaching challenged the surrounding culture. Despite some movement for equal rights, the oppression of women prevailed and their emancipation had scarcely begun. The wife's position was one of legal incapacity which amounted to enslavement.

The notion, then, of the husband making sacrifices to bring his wife closer to perfection, of him putting her interests first, was almost totally new. To get the idea across Paul avoids a direct attack on the current, widely accepted legal position of women. That might have exposed him to ridicule, and Christians were in no position to change the law anyway.

Instead, he uses language and concepts which were acceptable to his readers, but gives them new meaning. The husband's headship no longer means authority, but completion. His love is to be like Christ's, which involved submission; Jesus became a servant. Rather than launching a frontal attack on the cultural enemy, Paul infiltrates his ideas between the lines. Headship was to be undermined from within.

The model of mutual submission between Christ and his family challenges marriage today. Many a husband will surrender his life to alcohol, or to the glamour of politics, or to money and ambition, or to his work long before he would think of surrendering it to his wife. But the husband is to put his wife first by spending time with her, by remarking on her qualities, by encouraging her, by not stereotyping her, by being generous with his money and by renouncing his attachment to her good looks as she grows old. The wife is to do the same.

It is sometimes said that mutual submission is impossible in practice. What happens when the couple disagree? Who is to make the decision? There is no need to assume that the husband must always decide. When the two become 'wedlocked', there is nothing to prevent the final decision alternating between them. ('We did it my way last time, let's do it your way now.') If the matter is serious, they can ask a friend to arbitrate, as it were. Or they can carve out separate spheres of responsibility – the wife will have the last word over the money, the husband will arrange the holiday (provided she pays!).

What is clear is that conflict will be handled more constructively if both sides submit to each other. It is very hard to row if both are saying, 'Let's do what you want.' 'Marriage at its best is a sort of contest in what might be called "one-downmanship", a backwards tug-of-war between two wills determined not to win.'[1] That is how Paul's view of equality should work in practice.

The old music hall joke quipped, 'Since I've left my wife behind me I've never looked back.' The Bible says that if we look forward to the finished work of Christ, we shall be less likely to leave our spouses behind.

Challenge to solidarity

In chapter 7 we saw how Israelite families were to help build God's glorious family, where relationships would be characterised by equality, solidarity and liberty. In chapter 10 we saw that equality is one of the hallmarks of the family created through the cross. So it is no surprise to find that a pivotal relationship within that family, the relationship between Jesus and his sisters and brothers (the Church), models equality in a way that profoundly affects marriage.

Solidarity is another feature of the family made possible by the cross. Again, it is a model that reaches from the past into the future. Just as the *go'el* in ancient Israel bought back relatives who had been sold into slavery, so the Son has acted as our *go'el*, our redeemer, to buy sinners back from slavery by

---

1. Mike Mason, *The Mystery of Marriage: As Iron Sharpens Iron*, p. 139.

means of the cross (Gal. 4:3ff). Hebrews 2:11 emphasises that, like the *go'el*, Jesus did this as a fellow member of the family – God's family, to which we now belong. He continues to stand by us through his Spirit, who unites us to himself and makes his help available to us.

Though believers are already one with Jesus and so with each other, this unity will not be experienced fully till the future when we shall be united with the Son in his resurrection (Rom. 6:5). Then all the divisiveness of sin will be abolished. We shall be bound together as one people, a single 'dwelling in which God lives by his Spirit' (Eph. 2:22). Only at the end of history will the voice from the throne be able to declare with emphatic finality, '. . . the old order of things has passed away' (Rev. 21:4).

This vision of the unity, the solidarity, that is the destiny of God's family inspired Paul to urge his fellow Christians to make that unity real on this earth. He pictures the church as a body which is built up as members serve each other, 'until we all reach unity in the faith. . .'. From Christ 'the whole body, joined and held together by every supporting ligament, grows and builds itself up in love, as each part does its work' (Eph. 4:13, 16).

Making this unity real in the early church must have strengthened families. For as people used their gifts to unite and build God's family, the unity of individual families would have been reinforced. One of the gifts in the body, for example, was teaching (Eph. 4:11). It is reasonable to assume that as this gift was exercised, parents and children would have been taught how to relate to each other in ways that built up the family. So families would have been taught to care for their dependent relatives (1 Tim. 5:4). At Colosse, presumably they would have been shown the implications of Paul's teaching about family life (Col. 3:18ff).

Unity in the church was to be expressed through family-like relationships, in which older men were to be treated as fathers and peers as brothers or sisters (1 Tim. 5:1f). These relationships must have provided models for individual families. So when church members encouraged, affirmed and accepted one another so as to promote a spirit of unity (Rom. 12:8, 10; 15:5, 7), individuals would have seen examples of how to do the same at home. Parents could have learnt something about leadership in the family from models of leadership within the church. Experiencing affirmation and support within the church would have enhanced, say, a single parent's sense of well-being, and given her strength to bring up her children.

That's why it is important today for families to share in the life of a church which is challenged by the unity all believers will one day enjoy. As church members seek to make that unity real in the present, families will be strengthened by their involvement. To take just one example: a church which is committed to being one family will avoid activities which consistently separate people into age-layers – the top of the cake for senior citizens, the icing in the middle for young mums, and the bottom layer for children and youth.

It will make room for some activities which slice the cake into segments involving all three layers – an all-age barn dance, weekend holidays, church picnics, and all-age worship for example. Intermingling the ages will challenge the modern expectation that the generations should be separate. People will learn to relate across the years, which will make a difference to what happens at home.

Families which have moved into the area will find support from a church that is doing these things. They will have a new set of 'relations', to compensate for those they've left behind. Opportunities will be discovered for families to support each other. Single people will feel at home in the wider family, and may find themselves drawn into – and enriching – particular homes.

So it is that the future – a family whose members are totally at one with each other in heaven – can be brought into the present. And as this unity is expressed in the church, solidarity within individual families will be reinforced.

The challenge to liberty

Liberty was to have been a third mark of the glorious family of Israel, and it is a characteristic of God's family created through the cross. The Son not only hung in our place so that we could become one with him now and even more so in the future: he died so that we could be completely free in the future.

This is underlined in Ephesians 5:25ff, the end of the passage we looked at earlier. Paul writes of Christ dying for the Church so that at the end of history he can present her to himself as holy, spotless and freed from all imperfection. One expositor has said,

> Dare I put it like this? The Beauty Specialist will have put his final touch to the church, the massaging will have been so perfect that there will not be a single wrinkle left. She will look young, and in the bloom of youth, with colour in her cheeks, with her skin perfect, without any spots or wrinkles. And she will remain like that for ever and ever.[2]

This vision of God's family freed from all defects includes being free from all kinds of oppression. Revelation contains a vision of this freedom being celebrated in heaven in worship. 'Worthy is the Lamb, who was slain', 'Salvation belongs to the Lamb' (Rev. 5:12; 6:10). Such is the praise that will be given at the end of history by men and women. They will rejoice in the abolition through the cross of all injustice, all disease and all personal failure – in the freedom of God's family from all wrong.

This future was brought into the present in the worship of the early church. The Lord's Supper became central. It was a celebration of the freedom from death and sin that was won on the cross. As a foretaste of the full enjoyment of this freedom in heaven, spiritual gifts – which themselves freed the church from some imperfections – were released in the context of eucharistic worship. Improper worship weakened their effectiveness (1 Cor. 11–14).

The future was also brought into the present in the moral outlook of the first Christians. Philemon was to receive Onesimus not as a slave, but as a free brother (Philem. 16). The socially disadvantaged were freed from destitution: widows in need were looked after; possessions were shared with the poor (Acts 4: 32ff; 1 Tim. 5:3).

Realising this vision in the church must have had an impact on families. The Lord's Supper provided a model for family worship. We are not told anything about this, but many of the first Christians were Jews who were accustomed to praying at home. It is inconceivable that their household prayers did not echo the new emphases and atmosphere of Christian worship.

---

2. D. Martyn Lloyd-Jones, *Life in the Spirit in Marriage, Home and Work, An Exposition of Eph. 5:18 to 6:9*. Banner of Truth, London 1974, pp. 175–6.

Other aspects of family life must also have been affected. It seems that the treatment of slaves as brothers became so accepted there was a danger slaves would regard themselves as equally free at home, a clear case of church influencing family. That is why Timothy was warned that slaves must continue to respect their Christian masters (1 Tim. 6:2). But equally masters were not to exploit their slaves. They were to treat them fairly (Col. 4:1). This was an astonishing innovation when slaves were regarded as things more than people.

Families were also warned against allowing their wealth to corrode justice (James 5:4ff). They were to care for their disadvantaged relatives (1 Tim. 5:4ff), and for the less fortunate outside the home. They were to provide strangers with hospitality and to remember those who were ill-treated (Heb. 13:2f). As in ancient Israel, they were to promote freedom from oppression.

That remains their task today as they are confronted by the model of God's family in heaven, liberated from all defects. Families bring that future into the present when they care for dependent relatives and free them from some of the fear of growing old. They do so when their weaker members are treated fairly at home and freed from the risk of getting hurt.

The same happens when spouses and children are helped to realise their potential; freed from some of their limitations, they become more complete people. The future confronts the present when families are challenged to support those in need outside the home – when they devote some of their time, money or skills to working with the disadvantaged. It happens whenever the vision of God's glorious family provokes a concern for justice.

Not least, families can worship God in anticipation of worship in heaven. They are to be the church at home. They are to be inspired by the vision of heavenly worship to worship themselves. They are to learn from worship in the church what worship in the family can mean. Just as the Lord's Supper should encourage people to review their relationships with others (1 Cor. 11:28), so household prayers can be a time when the family reviews its relationships.

Just as the Lord's Supper celebrates God's forgiveness of sin, so family prayers can focus on God's forgiveness of domestic tensions and quarrels. Just as the Holy Spirit is invoked during the Eucharist, so his power can be experienced by the family.

Family worship can bring freedom from hurt, it can bring freedom in the Spirit, and it can strengthen the family to bring freedom to other people.

Edith Schaeffer has written out of her experience of family prayers.

> If it is to be prayer, it should not be superficial, but actual praying for needs of the family, for people the children ask prayer for – or whose needs you share with them . . . pray for cousins or playmates, people the child knows, and don't make it some sort of a pattern for them to follow, but real for *you*. Many a time my children have fallen to sleep as I've knelt by their beds praying for the very real needs of the moment.

She continues, perhaps reflecting a rather middle-class home,

> . . . The singing of hymns, choruses, and psalms, and songs with hand motions should be joyous times, around a piano if you have one, banging on triangles for little ones – and by recorders or violins if you have budding musicians. . . Marching around while banging on little drums or cymbals, little children should be singing, 'Dare to be a Daniel, Dare to stand alone!' They will be enjoying it like mad, but also, as time goes on, learning that standing alone like Daniel can be very real in their *own* lives, and the life of the family.[3]

Conclusion

In part 2 we saw how families were to create an international family which was loyal to God, and which reflected his glory by promoting equality, solidarity and liberty. We then saw that though Israelite families began the task by producing a home for the Messiah, they were totally unable to complete it. As a result, the Father and Son created the family themselves by means of the cross.

The last three chapters have shown how this family contains models which found echoes in the first Christian homes, and which still challenge families today. Families are challenged to be outward-looking, to develop parent–child relationships

3. Edith Schaeffer, *What is a Family?* Highland Books, Crowborough 1975, pp. 38–9.

based on what is being modelled by the Father and the Son, and to foster equality within marriage as well as solidarity and liberty at home. As families meet this challenge, they will contribute to God's global and glorious family. Models from the future will have helped them to achieve in the present what God had intended in the past.

How does all this help the family to cope with the pressures discussed in part 1?

PART FIVE
Hopeful families

13

Healing values

A study of sixty-five couples married in 1979 found that marriages were most likely to fail if the partners were uncertain, aimless and passive, if they ambled from day to day instead of seeking to achieve goals. Their happy-go-lucky approach worked against the effort, self-denial, patience, tolerance, kindness and generosity – mixed with humour and fun – needed to build an enduring relationship.[1]

Earlier we saw how the self-please ethic, a strong feature of our society, discourages commitment to family. It allows individuals to focus on themselves rather than other people. It comes too close to selfishness to prevent the selfishness which hurts families. The answer to this ethic is for families to have goals (not so that they can be managed like a business, but so that they can have a vision), and for these goals to arise from a morality which has a strong future direction.

Scripture's approach, which has that dimension, puts a far tighter armlock round the impulses that wreck families than the self-please ethic can ever achieve. It creates an atmosphere that promotes better family life. It injects insights, teaches new patterns of behaviour and provides reasons for change. Sometimes this alone will produce more healthy families. When it's not enough and families need help from outside, intervention will be more effective if families share the biblical view.

Future first

One of the problems with the self-please morality is that it undermines commitment to relationships. It puts an accent on

1. Penny Mansfield and Jean Collard, *The Beginning of the Rest of Your Life*. Macmillan, London 1988.

the individual who is seen as autonomous, as being under no authority except her own. Her personal needs are more important than family ties. This allows her to treat the family unfairly. She may put unreasonable demands on her husband or neglect the children.

The Bible encourages a far stronger commitment to relationships. Recent surveys have found that many people in Britain think that the best years of their lives were those in which they shared the experience of war. What colours the bombing of cities, the shortages of food and the constant presence of death is the memory of a shared commitment to a common cause.

People will always bind together if the goal is important enough. The Bible provides a goal for family life that is of supreme importance. It is to create God's family. Instead of doing their own thing, as the self-please view encourages, family members are to unite behind that goal. Relationships become immensely important because it is through them that the goal is attained.

It is a goal which puts the future ahead of the present. The self-please ethic thrives on pleasure now. It doesn't necessarily see marriage as a binding commitment. And when it does it may well lack the impetus to sustain it, because its focus is on each of the partners' immediate self-fulfilment: they can walk out of the marriage if they find a faster lane to pleasure. It also allows parents to neglect their children while they seek fulfilment in the here and now.

By contrast, the Bible puts the future of God's family first. Families have not been created mainly to seek immediate pleasure: they are to build God's world-wide community which will be completed in heaven. That is their goal, and they can look steadily toward it because they have been captivated by it.

It is a goal which brings the future into the present. Our identity is not rooted in our past families, nor in our current search for fulfilment through work, hobbies or a new marriage. We have been adopted into God's family, which we have yet to experience in its full splendour. So we see ourselves not through our parents' eyes (what they expected of me), nor through our partner's eyes (what he or she expects of me), nor yet through our own eyes (what we expect of ourselves).

Rather, we see ourselves through the eyes of the future, in terms of 'our family', God's family, the family of the future, and in terms of the demands that family makes on us. As a son I am to identify with the heavenly Son who will hand back the Kingdom, as a father with the heavenly Father who all through history delegates authority to his Son, and as a husband with my brother Jesus who will perfect his bride. Identifying with the future will affect my life in the present.

It is a goal which makes the future more real than the present. The self-please ethic feeds off the present because very often it has no hope in the future. It won't make sacrifices for the future because it has little vision of what the future will hold. Frequently it looks at the world as if it was a picture in a frame. Yet God has taken off the frame and extended the picture. Now the picture includes the future as well as the present. We can see how existing families will disappear, but God's family will last for ever. The present appears transient, the future permanent. Because it is more permanent, it becomes more real.

By putting the future ahead of the present, bringing the future into the present and making the future more real than the present, the goal of family life has the power to change behaviour. The vision of what God's family will be like becomes immensely important. It challenges families to embrace the values of God's family. Unlike the self-please ethic, it helps to restrain the impulses which cause pain in the treatment of children and in marriage.

Justice toward children

The parents of a disturbed girl sat down in the therapist's room. Mother put her bag on the chair next to her. The daughter began walking round the room, picking up objects here and there and staring inquisitively at them. 'Sit down!' her father said. The girl took no notice. 'Sit down!' he said again. Still she took no notice. 'Hey, look here!' His voice rose. There was a pause. . . Without a word mother took her handbag off the chair, and immediately the girl sat next to her. Unwittingly, it seemed, mother and daughter had once more undermined the man's authority.

This was a family which displayed the rejection and clinging tendencies which we highlighted in chapter 4. Mother apparently had become so used to clinging to her daughter that together they were acting as a team. Their team-work had slowly destroyed the husband's self-respect. To get even, the husband would alternate between withdrawing from the family, and then laying down the law in an outburst of rage. Violence toward children was part of the family's story. They felt thoroughly rejected by him – and he by them.

Against rejection

In the next thirty minutes, 285 children will become victims of broken homes in the United States and most will feel devastated, 685 teenagers will take some form of narcotics and 57 children will become runaways.[2] Two family therapists have written, 'Perhaps no age has mass-produced children who grow up without responsible parenting on as large a scale as our own . . . children are being mass-produced by parents who do not intend or are emotionally unable to care for them.'[3] This has much to do with the self-please ethic, which as we've seen creates a moral atmosphere that encourages the neglect of children.

Scripture's approach to parenting makes the child count, because it gives parents a clear goal. They are to raise children who can make an informed choice about whether to contribute to God's family, and who are equipped to make that contribution. Parenting is to help build the Father's family. This requires parents to make a commitment to their children. They are to pass on to each child the values of God's family. That means they must spend time with the child, which will show that he or she is valued by them. What destroys a child's sense of worth, as much as anything, is to have a father who never takes any notice.

Parents are to teach their children within a relationship of love. We saw in chapter 12 how the Father has modelled this love in relation to his Son. It involves the provision of security, praise and recognition, the giving of responsibility, and two-way communication which is honest and frequent. That kind of love is costly. It requires time and sacrifice. The higher the cost, the more valued the child.

Parental love is to be supported by discipline, which shows that the child's behaviour matters to his mother and father – it

2. Quoted by Josh McDowell, 'The Gap Widens', *Eternity*, June 1987, p. 19.
3. Ivan Boszormenyi-Nagy and Geraldine M. Spark, *Invisible Loyalties. Reciprocity in Intergenerational Family Therapy*. New York 1973, p. 40.

is sufficiently important to be worth punishing. That will send a message that the child matters. The child will grow up feeling affirmed rather than rejected.

Against clinging

At the other extreme, we've noted how the self-please ethic comes too close to self-interest to prevent parents clinging to their child so as to meet their deep-seated needs. Parents who are afraid of change, for example, may cling to a child to prevent him growing up. Mother may hold on to a mental picture of her son as a young boy, and treat him as such, even though he has become an adolescent. She is trying to obliterate 'the face of the biological clock' to hide the evidence of change. But her son will feel trapped and stifled.

The Bible, by contrast, encourages parents to let their children go. In the Old Testament the husband was to leave his parents and cleave to his wife. In the New Testament Jesus separates from his parents. It is made clear that the Father has delegated authority to his Son. Parents are to raise a child who can separate from them, so that she can identify not with her home but with God's family.

The Bible provides a structure in which parents can encourage each other to do this. The Old Testament expects parents to act as a team. Though not too much should be read into it, this oneness is reinforced by the model of parenting provided by the Father: mothering and fathering are so much a joint task that the Father combines both in his one person. Parents today are to be united so that their team-work reflects this oneness. When that happens, the Father's image (singular) will be displayed by the man and the woman together – plural (Gen. 1:27).

This team approach can prevent parents becoming over-involved with their children. An anxious mother, alone with her baby for much of the day, can become too protective toward him. She may cling to him in a suffocating way. But the father, coming back in the evening, can be more objective. He can provide emotional support which eases her worry, and helps her to let go a little.

A classic American study of emotionally healthy families found that family members were less likely to cling to each other if they had a source of meaning outside the family. If all that was important in life were immediate relatives, then members would be inclined to hang on to each other – and stifle one another – lest the family grow apart. But if meaning came from outside the home, they found it easier to respect each other's separateness.[4]

The faith of the Bible provides that meaning. It is a meaning that is rooted in the future. The future is to confront the present to bring change. If parents are committed to that idea, they will be alert to what is new. They will be open to change in their relationships with their children. They will be less inclined to cling to a child in the hope that the present will be preserved.

Parents who are motivated by the goal of creating God's family will have less chance of rejecting their children on the one hand or clinging to them on the other. They will be more likely to raise a child who will separate from his parents without feeling resentful toward them. Even if he abandons their beliefs, he will know that he was valued and fairly treated.

Justice in marriage

Against rejection

Newly-weds may be shocked to find how quickly romantic love is exhausted, how soon the quarrels start and how many of their needs – to be fulfilled through work, to pursue hobbies, to gossip with like-minded friends or to watch the ball game – have to be met outside marriage. Sometimes these interests take so much time that the partners pursue separate lives and drift apart. Much later, when their children have left home, husband and wife may look at each other and ask, secretly, 'Why did I marry you?'

Best-selling American author, Maggie Scarf, described a couple who came to dinner while she and her husband were in Los Angeles.

> They arrived from Las Vegas by car, and she was wearing a quilted dressing gown. I was so surprised I literally didn't know what to say, so I said, 'Are you expecting?' She said, 'Well, yes I am.' The husband said, 'What?!!!!' I said, 'How

---

4. Jerry M. Lewis et al., *No Single Thread: Psychological Health in Family Systems*, p. 70.

far along are you?' She said, 'Four months'. Said the husband, 'Why didn't you tell me?' And she said, 'Why didn't you ask me?'[5]

In 'let go' marriages like this one partner may be so preoccupied with being fulfilled outside the home that he has no time for his spouse; she feels neglected and hard done by. Or else the partners let go because they are unable to build each other up; both feel rejected by the other. In many of these cases the partners' emotional needs are so great that no morality is enough, on its own, to cement the marriage. The couple need the love and wise counsel of friends and perhaps experts.

The future focus of Scripture, however, is of much more help than the self-please ethic. Partners will enter marriage not mainly because they are seeking their own fulfilment, but because they feel called to the state of matrimony itself. They will have a commitment to the institution of marriage, as well as a love for each other. And the basis of that commitment will be the goal of marriage – to contribute to God's family. Husband and wife will try to bring out the best in each other so that they can make God's family more present on earth.

My wife says that the way I have affirmed her over the years (which is not so difficult when you believe in the other person) has given her the confidence to try things now that she would never have dreamed of doing in the past. She would say that she is proof that Ephesians 5 works. For what the husband does in the present will have an effect on the future. If he puts his wife's interests first today he will bring out the best in her tomorrow. And of course the same happens – as I know from experience – when it's the other way round, when the wife submits her desires now to the future potential of her husband.

By submitting to each other, husband and wife accept what God has given to the other person, and that acceptance allows the person's gifts to flourish. They commit themselves to what their partner can become through marriage, and to what that becoming will do for God's family. Behaviour that in any case should be motivated by love is also dictated by the future. There is a double reason for affirming, rather than rejecting, one another.

---

5. *The Guardian*, 17 May 1988.

Against clinging

At the opposite extreme are 'lean to' marriages, where a partner clutches hold of her spouse and traps him. The wife may be terrified by loneliness. When her husband goes to the pub, he triggers all her fears of being abandoned. Her protests leave the man resentful at how his freedom has been curtailed.

Or the husband may see his wife as an extension of himself. He fails to respect her as a separate person. He assumes that her needs are the same as his. He fuses himself so tightly to her that she cannot shine as a person in her own right. All the time she must do what her husband wants.

Commitment to what the partner can become in the future will encourage the spouses to keep an appropriate emotional distance. The husband will be less likely to interpret his wife's needs in terms of his own, which the self-please ethic may encourage by failing to put a firm moral boundary around his needs. Instead he will ask her how she can be freed to contribute to the future. He won't try to make her into what he would like her to be.

He will stand back, and from the vantage point of God's family ask, 'What are her gifts? What contributions can she make? How can I draw out what is distinctively her?' He will respect her separateness. And his wife will do the same. Releasing each other's potential requires the partners not to intrude but to give one another space.

Salvador Minuchin, a doyen of American family therapy, has argued that husbands and wives should settle their differences by mutual surrender to each other. They should accept each other's distinctives and avoid trying to change the other person.

> The couple must develop patterns in which each spouse supports the other's functioning in many areas. They must develop patterns of complementarity that allow each spouse to 'give in' without feeling he has 'given up'. . . In the process of mutual accommodation, spouses may actualise creative aspects of their partners that were dormant and support the best characteristics of each other.[6]

Partners are not to manipulate one another. They are not to impose their ambitions on each other. They are to respect each

---

6. Salvador Minuchin, *Families and Family Therapy*, p. 56.

other by drawing out the best in one another – for the sake of the future.

Here then is a morality which promotes family welfare. 'But what is the dynamic for change?', one person asked after reading this. 'How can we live up to these Christian ideals and make them true in our experience?' The answer lies in what chapter 10 said about the Holy Spirit. It is he who brings us into God's family, like a divine midwife who makes possible new birth, and who bonds us into that family. Just as a parent–child bond involves the communication of values from parent to child, so the Holy Spirit communicates the Father's values to us. Gradually he implants them in our minds and changes our attitudes. Bit by bit the morality of God's family becomes our morality.

One way he does this is by helping us to identify with God's family – to see it as *my* family. If I 'own' the family, I'm more likely to own its values. He also encourages us to learn from the examples of others in this family. We can see how to put these values into practice. A third way is by giving us the emotional energy to make the necessary changes. We actually make the effort. These important themes are taken up in the next chapter.

One of Britain's agony aunts, Inma Kurtz, has written,

> Binding contracts are made every day without any detached counsel, based on an emotion which is by definition ephemeral, and signed by two people who are not in their right minds (in love is questionably a form of temporary insanity). No intelligent person would set up a corner shop in such manner, let alone a household and a new line in human beings.[7]

The Bible has a less jaundiced view of love, but it too recognises love's limitations. Feelings of love alone cannot meet all the demands of parenting or marriage. They need reinforcing by a strong framework of morality. That's why Scripture provides a moral purpose to sustain families when love grows cold, or when – in the heat of the moment – love is unwise.

---

7. Inma Kurtz, *Malespeak*. London 1986, p. 64.

14

Healing the past

Dr Kenneth McAll, a consultant psychiatrist, has described the case of Margaret who began, aged 73, to have violent outbursts of temper, unprovoked aggression toward her sister with whom she lived, and bouts of smashing objects. Her mother had behaved in a similar way. Further investigation showed that not just her mother, but for the past six generations the eldest female in the family had shown signs of similarly disturbed behaviour.[1]

We saw in chapter 3 how family pain is often 'kin deep' – it is passed from one generation to the next. That is frequently because families don't expect to change, or don't want to change, or don't know how to change, or don't have the energy to change – or a combination of all these. Families are often bound by destructive rules of which they are scarcely even aware.

By contrast, Scripture expects family health to be handed down the generations, and it has provided an alternative set of rules – not legalism, but a way of life – which can enable that to happen. These rules are above-board and are a matter of choice. The aim of parenting is to raise children who will choose for themselves whether to follow their parents' example. So whereas hurts are largely imposed by being passed unconsciously from one generation to the next, the biblical ideal is that each generation should have the freedom to choose whether to walk in 'the paths of righteousness'.

The way of liberation, then, is for families to break free – as far as possible – from the hidden rules which trap them in unfairness. In 1 Peter 1:18 it declares that we have been 're-deemed from the empty way of life handed down to you from

1. Kenneth McAll, *Healing the Family Tree*. London, SPCK, 1982, pp. 13–15.

your forefathers' thanks to the cross. We have been set free from the 'empty' rules which we have inherited from our families.

We can experience some of that freedom on this earth because through the cross God has established the family that human homes were unable to create on their own. Since the future of that family is guaranteed therefore (it does not depend solely on human achievement), individual families can seek to contribute to it; their work will not be wasted. At the same time, they can learn from models within it. Particular families may still need outside help to change their harmful behaviour, but they will find that change easier if they are committed to God's family.

Expecting to change

It has been said that you can take a child out of his family, but you can't take his family out of the child. A child may imbibe his family's rules and reproduce them in the home he creates partly because he has no real expectation of change. He may have been brought up in a home where the rules were rigid, and which leaves him insecure in a less controlled environment. To compensate for his own insecurities, he repeats what he is used to and rules his home with a rod of iron. His own children in turn will find it hard to live outside an authoritarian framework, and may behave in the same way toward their children. There will be no change partly because no one expects it.

Expectancy of change, however, is at the heart of the Bible's view of the family. The Old Testament portrays families on the move. Adam and Eve were to have a family that would move out of the garden to create a global family. Abraham left home to create a godly family, in which his knowledge of God would be passed to his offspring. Spouses were to pull away from the legal position of women to create a more glorious equality. Jesus separated from his earthly parents to identify with his heavenly Father.

In the same way, we are to move out of home emotionally to identify with God's family. That must be one of the biggest psychological changes that a person can experience – so much so that Jesus described it as a new birth. It involves casting off from the safe existence we already have and opting for a new and richer life outside the womb of security, parental expectations, possessions or whatever surrounded our life till then.

It involves seeing the present from the standpoint of the future. We look at our families from the point of view of what they are to become and ask, 'What needs to be changed? Are we too inward looking as a family? Have we abdicated our teaching role as parents? Are we remiss as adult children? Are we failing to submit in our marriages?' As we cling to the future we shall be less inclined to cling to the present.

Joy's marriage was crumbling. She resented Derek because he gave more time to his woodwork and to his job than he did to her. But somehow they could never talk about the problem, which only added to Joy's nagging sense that something was missing in her life. 'It was as if I was hungry, but didn't know what to eat.'

One day, after a long period of searching, she became a Christian. Her husband noticed that she became more open. 'I found that she was sharing her feelings with me in a way she hadn't before. It was very threatening, actually. Because I had to face the fact that she was angry with me. But at the same time I could see that she was becoming more honest and open with her friends. Her friendships moved on to a greater depth. It set me thinking.' Four years later Derek, too, became a Christian. He wanted to be open like his wife to help their marriage survive. He had acquired an expectation of change.

Wanting to change

Families also need the desire to change. Normally families will stick with their rules, however painful, because they're afraid that change will be even more distressing. The family scapegoat may fear that if he stops being blamed he will no longer be noticed. Members of the family hang on to the present (or past) because they are in despair about the future.

The biblical view of family challenges that despair. It builds confidence in the future by underlining its reality. Though imperfectly experienced now, God's family has already been established. The failure of earthly families to bring it into existence has been overcome on the cross. Human families will disappear, but God's family will last for all eternity and earthly families can make a contribution to it.

This gives life a sense of purpose and meaning. If a person can plug into a feeling that existence is going somewhere, then despite the bad things that happen to her she can still feel that the universe is basically 'all right'. Things will work out eventually, so she can face life with more confidence. Observation of healthy families suggests that people who are optimistic about life don't depend so heavily on meaning derived from a particular person. They will feel less need to hold on to the person in an attempt to preserve the present.[2] They will be more willing to change.

The biblical view challenges despair by suggesting that the benefits of change do, indeed, outweigh the advantages of staying still. There is the benefit of having more in common with the Father and the Son by becoming more like them in our approach to parenting, in respecting our own father and mother and in the treatment of our spouse. Since it is God's purpose that we should become like him, we can anticipate the reward of hearing, 'Well done, my good and faithful servant'.

There are other rewards. God established a pattern of family life that was designed to create God's family. So the approach to parenting was meant to produce children who by honouring their parents would discover God and experience his blessings; principles for marriage were designed to create a relationship around which would form a healthy family, concerned with justice and liberty; these families, by the very quality of their relationships, were to create a community in which God's glory would be revealed.

Now if God originally entrusted to families the task of building his family, then we can be sure that the principles he set out for family life were designed to work. They were designed to accomplish the purpose of building a perfect family. This means that the reward for changing our families is the knowledge that they will become more like God's family, and that our homes will experience some of the joys of that family as a result.

So building families that are open to outsiders will be demanding, but will produce the satisfaction of knowing that you have done something worthwhile; you may also have been appreciated by those who were drawn in. Mutual submission

---

2. Jerry M. Lewis et al., *No Single Thread: Psychological Health in Family Systems*, p. 70.

in marriage is likely to produce the reward of being appreciated by one's spouse. Biblical parenting may earn the respect of one's children. Honouring parents may produce the reward of reconciliation.

Eric felt gnawed away inside by resentment towards his mother and father. He sometimes felt like hitting out at other people as a way of getting even with his parents. In counselling, he was shown how forgiving his parents so that he could affirm them ('handing back the Kingdom') would reduce his resentment and the tension inside him. He did so, and found a new acceptance at home.

The biblical view of family encourages change by creating confidence in the future and holding out the prospect that change will be rewarded. The past imperfect makes the present tense: the future perfect changes the present tense.

Knowing how to change

Families which want to change often have to be shown how to. Family therapists see that as part of their work. In a family where the members reject each other, for example, two therapists may join the family, but with one remaining silent. When her colleague makes a mistake, the silent therapist has a word with him outside the room.

After they return, the first therapist allows the second to explain to the family why she thinks her colleague is wrong. The 'rejected' therapist looks duly contrite, and acknowledges his error. This tactic delivers a blow to the family system by showing a peaceful redefinition of a one-up-one-down relationship.

The therapists in that situation provide a model – an example which has the power to produce change. All of us have grown up copying models in our own families. Some of these will have been helpful, but others will have encouraged behaviour that is damaging. New models can help us to break free from defective old ones.

God's family provides models of singleness, an open family, the Father–Son relationship, mutual submission in marriage, family solidarity and family concern for justice and liberty. These models can help to free us from the damaging models that have influenced us in our families.

HEALING THE PAST

Someone might say, 'But the models in God's family are invisible. We can only know them impersonally, through the pages of Scripture. How can they have the power to free us from models which we have seen and which have been emotionally close to us?'

One thing that makes human models effective is our ability to identify with them. This will be partly because in some way we feel they belong to us. The systemic closeness of the family gives me a sense that my parents are mine (they are 'my' parents). Because they are so important to me, I will take more notice of them than the couple next door. Equally, I will only copy what they do if it is not too remote. A little child will hardly try in real life to copy his father water-skiing, though he may use a toy to attempt an imitation in the more 'realistic' setting of his bath.

In a similar way, it is possible for believers to identify with the models in God's family. Having been adopted into the family, we belong to the Father and Son and they to us. What the family does matters because it is now 'our' family. The family will seem especially important because it will outlast our earthly families. The Holy Spirit, working at our conscious and unconscious levels to sanctify us, brings us into this family and makes us one with it (1 Cor. 12:13). He brings the models home to us.

Furthermore, the Father and Son are not remote from us. They have felt the pain of our human experience. The Father knows the parental agony of releasing a child to become a rebel. The Son has felt the little child's anguish of feeling abandoned by the parent on whom he totally depends. The Son knows what it is like to be the family scapegoat. He has experienced in acute form the cost involved in opening the Father–Son family to include (sinful) outsiders. He chose the way of equality and solidarity when he died to bring liberty to that family.

So the Father and Son understand the costs for us in copying the models in their family. They have felt intensely the type of pain we may experience – the pain perhaps of opening our families to outsiders and receiving few thanks or outright rejection in return, or the cost of sacrifice as we submit to the interests of our spouse or stand alongside a relative in need.

They have experienced the effects of a fallen world, and modelled the key relationships within God's family in that setting. They have brought the heavenly family into our world, and demonstrated that its role models can still work. They have overcome all those forces of self-interest which would say that it is too painful to release one's child, too painful to become independent and yet remain loyal to one's parents after being rejected by them, too painful to give way to one's husband or wife, too painful to support relatives in need – too painful, in fact, to strive to create a healthy family.

By experiencing these costs themselves, the Father and Son have saved their family models from being remote. They have made them realistic and brought them 'down to earth'. The models have become accessible to us. Research suggests that people are less willing to learn from models if they feel no empathy with them.[3] The Father and Son have made it possible for us to empathise – to identify – with their models.

Yet to copy someone, you still need to see them; an apprentice needs to see the craftsmen at work. Models in God's family need to be seen if they are to be an effective means of learning. That seeing can occur within the church, as we saw in the last chapter. When Christian families mix together they can experience something of the richness of relationship that we shall enjoy in the heavenly family.

As gifts are exercised – of helping others, of encouragement, of serving, of contributing to the needs of others, of teaching, of leadership and of showing mercy for example (Rom. 12:6ff; 1 Cor. 12:27ff) – family members can learn how to behave in a similar way at home.

An adult who never knew unconditional love as a child but has experienced it in the church, and has seen Christian parents loving their children unconditionally, can learn from these examples how to love her own child. If she never saw her parents exercise authority firmly and fairly, she may discover helpful role models within the church. The church can provide examples of people filling out, and making concrete and specific, the family models portrayed in Scripture. It can show families how to change.

---

3. Martha A. Perry and M. Judith Furukawa, 'Modelling Methods', in Frederick H. Kanfer and Arnold P. Goldstein (eds.), *Helping People Change: A Textbook of Methods*, pp. 131–71.

Having the energy to change

In chapter 3 we saw that families may be unable to change because they lack the psychological energy required. Members may feel so fragile that they consume an unhealthy amount of energy protecting themselves. They can't face something new.

Adoption into God's family provides us with some of the energy needed to change. Our future status is brought into the present. Our status is that of forgiven sinners who have been made perfect: the reality is that we keep sinning. We have been given the status of sons (Rom. 8:15) in advance of being made like the Son (v. 29). This means that we have some of the benefits of the future family now.

The first is the knowledge that we are accepted. Pippa was a tense, single mother of two adolescents. Feeling rather unsure of herself, she tended to worry which made it difficult to let go of her children. They became more and more resentful of her nagging. One day she learnt what it meant to have God as a Father whom she could talk to and listen to each day, and who would give her the security she had sought in her husband. Instead of struggling on her own, she found that she could let go of things. 'It's up to you,' she would say.

As she released her children to the Father, she found that she could be more relaxed in day-to-day matters. She still faced all the trials of bringing up a family alone, but she worried less and nagged less. Feeling accepted by the Father helped her 'to hand over the Kingdom' to her children.

The second is belonging. It can be experienced through the fellowship of Christians, which provides a foretaste of the belonging we shall feel in heaven. Belonging to a warm network of relationships helps a person feel safe. That security is vital if he is to have the courage to change his behaviour. It will also give him energy to change. If he spends less time making himself secure, he will have more energy to explore something new.

Thirdly, there is the completing work of the Holy Spirit. He is the deposit who guarantees our inheritance, which is to be made perfect (Eph. 1:14; 5:26f). He provides a foretaste, in other words, of the completion we shall one day experience in heaven. That foretaste is partly expressed in the Spirit's healing power.

It is worth underlining the Spirit's key role in providing the dynamic for change. Many families get stuck in situations of acute hurt. They try all sorts of therapy but to no avail, and then they discover the healing work of the Spirit. He releases them from the situation and heals their pain. Kenneth McAll, whose theological interpretation of some of his cases may be open to question, provides a number of instances where the Spirit's healing was found to be especially present in the Eucharist.

He reports one case where:

> Harry had married the young receptionist in his mother's hotel, and the newly-weds continued to live in the hotel. His wife developed a severe depression which prevented her from sleeping. Finally, through a Eucharist . . . the bond between Harry and his mother was cut and she agreed to Harry and his wife moving out of the hotel to live in a cottage some distance away. As Harry was freed from his mother's control, he began to relate anew to his wife; she, in turn, was freed from her depressive illness. All three formed a new, unbreakable spiritual bond.[4]

If a family worships together, it will find that the Spirit's power is released not only in church, but directly at home. One of my joys has been to see God answering my children's prayers. When I asked them recently to give some examples, my ten-year-old said, 'There're millions!'

They included recovery for a family friend, finding a friend on holiday and fine weather while we moved house! Perhaps more important are the 'sorry' prayers we say together. It's difficult to harbour a grudge if you've heard the other person asking God to forgive them for hurting you. Through prayer the Spirit brings reconciliation home.

So it is that God's family can break in from the future and help modern families to expect to change, to want to change, to know how to change and to have the energy to change. We must be careful not to overstate the case. There will always be families which need expert support. The powers of this world will always constrain the potential for change.

But families who live under the influence of God's family will have more than an ethic: they will have a way of life which, empowered by the Spirit, will give them the ability to change.

---

4. Kenneth McAll, *op cit.*, p. 21.

They will find themselves more able to exchange their damaging rules of behaviour for those that are healthy. A community shaped by the future will change the lives of families who enter its influence – and changed families will help to build the community of the future.

15

Healing society

> Peter's wife: 'I never see Peter.'
> Peter's children: 'We never see Dad.'
> Peter: 'I'm doing it for the wife and kids.'

Many a boy has watched the pleasure his father seems to receive from work – the time he puts into it and the way it preoccupies him – and concluded that achievement is the route to pleasure. So he struggles to achieve as an adult. He devotes himself to his job. Like his father, he neglects his children in the relentless pursuit of success. Just as his father felt anxious about failure, so does the son. But unfortunately, the son lacks the ability to do as well as his father. He becomes frustrated and demoralised, which increases tension in the marriage. Work deals the family a double blow.

In from the edge

In chapter 2 we saw how work has pushed families to the edge of modern society, and how this has led to painful responses at home. For example parents may neglect their children because they are bound up with their jobs, while the creation of a mothering role distinct from paid work has made it easier for women who become anxious and are at home much of the day to smother their children emotionally.

The Bible challenges the priority of work in modern society. The first man and woman were placed in the garden in a family relationship more than a work one. They were given a job to do, but it was given to them in the context of family. Adam was given more than a workmate: he received a 'one flesh' marital companion. Their offspring were to spread over the world to create a family rather than just a work community.

HEALING SOCIETY

Likewise the community Israel was to create is not described in terms of work, but of a nation with family characteristics. Family words, 'house' and 'people' (the Hebrew word originally referred to close relatives), were used of the nation because the people thought of themselves as a family. The task of building this national family was delegated not to work groups operating separately from home, but to families.

It is possible, of course, that this simply reflects the pre-industrial culture of ancient Israel, and that not too much should be read into it. Yet our approach all along has been to look for Old Testament themes which are echoed in the New. Perhaps, therefore, it is significant that in the New Testament God's family is saved not through work but through the cross, which involved a family relationship. The relationship was not between master and servant, a work relationship, but between the Father and the Son. The 'work' of the cross occurred in a family context.

And it created a family rather than just a work community. Relationships in the Kingdom are between brothers and sisters, and between the Father and his children. That is not to say that work is unimportant. After all God never stops working (John 5:17), and since we are made in his image presumably we shall go on working too. In the vision of the future given in Revelation 21, heaven is pictured as a civilisation, the New Jerusalem. Since work has always been an essential part of civilisation, there seems to be an implication that work will still be important in heaven.

But this work will be carried out within a set of family relationships. We shall relate to each other as sisters and brothers, not as masters and servants, managers and managed. Our work will not compete with family. It will be done inside our 'Father's house'. People will work from a heavenly home.

What all this does is to challenge not the notion of work, but the modern priority given to work. It means that it is appropriate for families today to feel the tension between work and home. Sometimes people are aware of this tension and feel guilty about it. So they either deny the problem ('I give the family lots of time at weekends' when that is not true), or they rationalise it ('I do my best' or 'It's not *that* bad'), or they refuse to talk about it at all.

Scripture lifts some of this guilt from individuals. For the conflict between work and home is not entirely their fault. It largely reflects social pressures outside the family, and this in turn reflects society's abandonment of the biblical ideal. Work was not to be in competition with home. So if we feel the tension, it is because society has lost God's vision and we are experiencing the results.

There is no need, therefore, to be over-harsh on ourselves. If we cannot spend the time we ought to with our families, we are not totally to blame. So we can afford to acknowledge reality and express how we feel. That will improve the situation. For children can live with their father being away a lot on business, or Mum on shifts, if they know their parents really wished they were at home. They find it much harder to cope if they suspect their parents are glad to be away. Expressing how we feel about the tension between work and home, and our own self-doubts about our preoccupation with work, will help the family to know that they really count.

Equally, the importance given to family in Scripture challenges us to put boundaries round our work – to avoid, if possible, excessive overtime at the expense of home, to make career decisions in the light of the family and to block out times for the family each day (or each week). This will create more time for the husband to join his wife (or vice versa) in parenting as a team. He will have more chance, perhaps, to provide that objectivity which will help the mother to avoid anxiously overclinging to her child. The family is too important to God not to be given its proper place.

The woman's place

In chapter 2 we saw how pushing the family to the edge of work reinforced the position of women in the family: they were on the edge of justice. Even with the huge changes in the status of women over the past hundred years, they still carry unfair burdens within the home. Working wives do the bulk of the housework, and where tasks are shared wives tend to do the less interesting ones.

God's family encourages partners to give to each other in marriage. They are to avoid the view of traditionalists, who say the family rules out feminism because authority rests with the man. Equally, they are to avoid the other extreme which says that feminism rules out the family. In their war on patriarchy, radical feminists have condemned the family as a vehicle for male dominance.

The biblical view allows us to say that aspects of feminism complete the family. Feminism's concern for equality and justice chimes with God's vision for family, and families are incomplete – they are less than they ought to be – when they do not share that concern. In ancient Israel marriages were very much part of a patriarchal culture. Yet the Old Testament contained seeds which would have challenged that culture. The family at the end of history, God's family, shows no preference for 'masculine' over 'feminine' traits; they seem to combine equally within both Father and Son.

The path to equality in the New Testament is very different to what is mapped out by most secular feminists. They tend to speak about the rights of women and how they can be freed to enjoy those rights. They talk about self-fulfilment, self-achievement and self-growth as desirable ends, apparently forgetting that it was men pursuing their self-fulfilment and their self-achievement which encouraged the ill-treatment of women to start with.

The New Testament does not follow this 'self-please' approach. It presents the Son giving up his 'masculine' place of authority next to the Father, so that he could submit himself – a stereotyped 'female' quality – to the cross. Paul uses this model of submission to encourage husbands and wives not to pursue their self-interests, but the interests of their spouses. Marriage will then become a means of making the partners more complete as people.

Scripture avoids spelling out what this will mean in very specific terms. There are no rigidly prescribed roles, no details about how responsibilities are to be divided, no stereotyped notions about what it means to be a father or mother. Husband and wife are to work as a team, bringing out creatively the best in each other and in their children. They are free to assign tasks and adopt roles in whatever way is best for the family as a whole.

The father is free to stay at home and look after the children and the wife to go out to work, or vice versa. The husband is free to do a paid job while his wife looks after the home. It is equally open for both of them to work and to share the domestic chores. The specifics will vary from home to home because married couples will differ. The overriding principle, however, is that partners must treat each other fairly by putting the interests of the other first.

In from the cold

Families are specially vulnerable to the breakdown of community. The mother who is isolated and tired will have few reserves of energy. Her temper will be frayed, her battered baby the only lightning conductor available for her frustrated exhaustion.

Building community is at the heart of the Bible's vision for families. The purpose of the Old Testament family was to help create God's family, and extended families (which were communities in themselves) were to do this by contributing to the life of the village, tribe and nation. An extended family is what was created on the cross. There, the Father and Son opened up their family to include outsiders who had done it harm. New Testament families expressed tangibly the open nature of this family. They allowed their households to become extended into 'the household of faith'.

Families build community today when they stand by their relatives in need. In so doing, they will strengthen social bonds as well as family ties. At a local level, what happens in the next block will become important because an uncle lives there. Nationally, what happens in Glasgow will be seen as significant because an aunt is there. As relatives become more concerned about each other, they will become more involved with society.

They will be likely to have particular concern for those who live on their own, not least the elderly. In the past forty years the number of Britons past retirement age has leapt from one in ten to nearly one in five. At the same time the family has been held up as a model of care. As far as possible, people should be cared for 'in the community' – they should be looked after by their families. This has been seen as warmer and more personal than large institutions.

In practice this has put great pressure on women to provide the care, and this pressure is likely to grow as the number of elderly continues to rise into the next century. Women are likely to feel trapped between their desire to work, the needs of their immediate family and the needs of an aging relative. Many will be unable to face the thought of an elderly relation moving in, even if they have the space. But a few minutes a week writing a letter or making a phone call can make all the difference. It can give a sense of value or belonging to someone on their own.

If families are to be effective agents of care they need help. They need adequate domiciliary services. If a person curtails their work to look after a dependent relative, they need reasonable financial support. The carer may also need practical and emotional support from friends in the neighbourhood. In other words, families need the support of the community if they are to help build community through their caring role.

Families will build community not only when they stand by their relatives, but when they stand by each other. Christian Weaver is pastor of the Pilgrim Holiness Church in Nottingham, England. The church contains people of mainly West Indian descent. He has described how the church is trying to recreate a sense of belonging to a wider family in which each person is valued.

Members are encouraged to spend time with each other mid-week,

> so that we can really live with each other and get on each other's nerves and discover what being a Christian means in coping with all that. It means that many people take part in parenting our children again and helping them in life. For example, sometimes people will come to the church who were baptised in the Islands and they had no idea who their Godparents are. They have lost touch with them. So within the church they will adopt a new Godfather and Godmother.
>
> Single people are often encouraged to link up with other families. We are often in each other's homes. We will share meals... Sunday lunch ... with each other and there is positive encouragement to welcome single people into the family. We deliberately try to break down any exclusiveness on the part of the nuclear family.

Families are encouraged not always to sit with each other, but to mix with others in the pews.[1]

Joan King, a family expert with Scripture Union in Britain, has coined the phrase 'community parenting' to describe how

---

1. Christian Weaver, 'The Family: a Caribbean Perspective', *Christian Impact*, 2 (Spring 1987), pp. 4–5.

church members might open their homes to their children's friends. They might have them in for Sunday lunch, involve them in family outings, even take them on the odd holiday, provided their parents agreed. These youngsters, many of whom may have very little family life, could then grow up not only playing in the street, but having something of a home. They would be shown a model of Christian parenting.

This is an example of how families, working together to build community, can have an impact on the neighbourhood. 'Being there' with God's vision for family, and standing alongside other families which share that vision, can lead to action which will make a difference to the area. It can lead to the setting-up of crèche facilities for working Mums, of call-in centres for the bereaved, of advice centres for those in trouble, or to joint approaches to the authorities so that local amenities can be improved.

With so many fractured and lonely families in the cities and so many people living alone, families are called to create an extended Christian family in which believers and outsiders alike can find a home. They are to create 'base communities' which can transform society bottom-up.

Confronting poverty

In particular, families are to combat the poverty which is a major cause of family injustice. Debbie, for example, was a bright little girl who lived with her mother in a damp basement room in one of London's bed-and-breakfast hotels. Like thousands of young children in central London, she could not remember, at the age of six, a home of her own. Her mother shared a kitchen with nine other families.

Though the family was very affectionate together, the strain of their cramped living conditions, their lack of privacy, mother's need to be out working all day (and some nights) and their meagre income, had begun to tell. Debbie had begun to use an asthma inhaler regularly. She and her sister would spend hours wandering around the nearby streets. Their mother was losing weight, largely because of the strain of eking out their slender budget.

In the Old Testament the family was to be a bulwark against poverty and oppression. As relatives stood by each other, and

HEALING SOCIETY

as families upheld a more or less equal distribution of wealth and power, they were to create a society in which justice prevailed. God's family created at the crucifixion keeps that vision alive: it promises an end to all poverty. Its values were given concrete expression by the first Christians, who shared their possessions to support the poor. Poverty remains a challenge today.

Families combat poverty by 'being there' as godly homes. More than half America's poor live in one-parent households, even though these homes comprise only sixteen per cent of all US families. Sixty per cent of divorced women with children in the UK depend on state benefits for a time. Marital breakdown is one of the major factors behind poverty today.[2]

Individuals inspired by God's view of the family will avoid getting married unless they feel called specifically to it. Once married, they will put the interests of their partner first. Though reasons for marital breakdown are complex, this biblical approach has the potential to reduce divorce – and the poverty that goes with it.

Families combat poverty when they join with other families to 'be there' with the poor – as did twenty-five members of the Bristol Christian Fellowship who sold up their homes, and moved out of the leafy suburbs into the 'inner city' area of St Paul's. This released substantial capital which was used to set up a people's centre for mums and children, and for people needing training, counselling, welfare advice, items of clothing and much security.

Families combat poverty by 'being there' in a concern for God's family. The more they identify with this family, the less inclined they will be to defend their narrow, sectional interests. They will have a wider view which will make them more sensitive to those in need. If you identify with your 'natural' family, then you will more likely pursue what is of advantage to your family. You will support mortgage-tax reliefs if you are a homeowner, tax-cuts if you are a wage-earner, child-benefit if you have children, private medicine if your family is insured.

But if you identify with God's wider family, which includes the rich and the poor, then you will support measures that benefit the family as a whole. You won't view these issues from

---

2. Stuart Butler and Anna Kondratas, *Out of the Poverty Trap*. New York 1987.

the standpoint of your own particular home, but from the vantage point of God's family. How can its values of equality, solidarity and liberty be made more real today?

That will affect how families talk about issues of wealth and poverty, how they vote in local and national elections, how much of their income they give to anti-poverty causes and how willing they are to get involved in local ventures to support the poor. Families with wealth and power which take these issues seriously, and which combine with other families, may be surprised at their impact on their neighbourhood – and the influence this will have on their elected representative at the national level.

By 'being there' as Christian families, using whatever opportunities they have to bring into the present something of God's promise for the future, families will promote justice in society. They will combat the temptations to put work first and women second. They will defend community and attack poverty. They will counter those pressures which hurt people at home. By acting for the world, families will also act for themselves.

16

Another view of family

'Bafflegab' is one of those interesting words which have been recently invented. It is defined by the Chambers Dictionary as: a profusion of abstruse technical terminology used as a means of persuasion, pacification or obfuscation. In other words, it makes perfect sense if you're an initiate, but it leaves the outsider totally confused. Theology is full of bafflegab! And that includes some of the terms which theologians have used to describe Christian teaching about families.

Models of the family

The sacramental view

Over the years there have been broadly two Christian models of the family. The Catholic one has been labelled the 'sacramental' view. This says that God pours out his grace in a specific way on believers, but also in a more general way on both believers and non-believers. This more general grace may incline a non-believer's heart toward God. Family, it is said, mediates this kind of grace. God becomes active in families to bring their members closer to him and closer to perfection.

So in marriage, all the couple have to do is to say ' "I will" – I will let God's activity break through in this holy sign of our mutual consent and our future life together', and God will bring some of his own love into their marriage. He will enable their love to rise above its natural limitations and acquire some of the characteristics of divine love. Marital love will display something of God's love to the world.[1]

---

1. Edward Schillebeeckx, *Marriage. Human Reality and Saving Mystery*; 'Marriage' in Karl Rahner et al. (eds.), *Sacramentum Mundi: An Encyclopedia of Theology*, pp. 414–8.

Likewise, grace is poured into the process of parenting. The couple will receive some of God's creative power in the act of procreation. They will receive some of God's love when they love their children. They will receive God's help to bring out the best in their children and in each other; God will help the child to bring out the best in parental love. Families will be brought closer to perfection.[2]

The family, then, is like a near empty cup which is filled with God's love and power so that God's love can be poured out to the world. When people look at family love, they see God's love. This comes quite close to the biblical view described in this book. In particular, it highlights how God's love is given to families not just for themselves, but for the world. It underlines, too, how at their best, families can bring their members a little closer to perfection.

The trouble with the Catholic view is that it can be easily misunderstood. It can be taken to mean that families receive grace automatically, so long as the couple are baptised and enter marriage with the right intentions. If the couple promise publicly, 'We will let God's love break into our marriage', the Catholic view can be understood as saying that this will automatically happen. Yet the brutal reality is that many marriages, created by baptised people with the best of intentions, are violent, emotionally destructive and don't last. It is hard to find God's grace in the wreckage that remains. The Catholic view is weak in showing *how* grace is poured into families.

The covenant view

Most strands of Protestant teaching about the family can be held together within the covenant model. This says that family relationships, at their best, imitate the covenant relationship between God and his people. They reflect aspects of God's covenant love.

G. R. Dunstan, for example, has drawn attention to five similarities between God's covenant with his people and the marriage relationship. First, there is an initiative of love which invites a response and creates a relationship (God reaches out to his people, a husband proposes to his wife). There is a public moral affirmation which secures the relationship (the Israelites

---

2. 'Pastoral Constitution on the Church in the Modern World', part 2, ch. 2, in Walter M. Abbott (ed.), *The Documents of Vatican II*, p. 252.

took an oath, the couple make a vow). There are obligations which undergird the relationship (the people were to keep the commandments, the couple are to remain faithful). Blessings are promised to the faithful (prosperity and long life to the Israelites, children to the couple). An element of sacrifice is involved (the sacrificial system in Israel, mutual submission in marriage).[3]

This model can be extended to include children. 'In a moral sense, what brings people together as a family is the covenant of loyalty to one another from birth to death.' Children are nurtured within 'a circle of covenanted care'.[4]

The great strength of this view is that it stresses the mutual obligations of family members, which is something that we have highlighted in relation to parents and children and to marriage. Its weakness is that, like the sacramental model, it can be easily misunderstood. It can be seen as not emphasising enough what the family is for, as not highlighting the family which human homes are to help create. Often it seems to present the family in a rather static way, with an accent on relationships in the here and now. We are not always encouraged to see families as being on the move.

An eschatological model

Eschatology is another one of those bafflegab words. It means 'last things', and the view of family presented in this book can perhaps be best described as eschatological. It's a future-first model because the stress is on where the family is going.

So we have emphasised the purpose of the family, as being to create a global family in which knowledge of God is passed from one generation to the next, and in which God's glory is reflected in relationships of equality, solidarity and liberty.

Human families have failed to achieve fully their purpose. Consequently, the Father and Son experienced the core pains of family life in order to create that family themselves. The cross required Jesus to choose the path of equality, solidarity and liberty, means which were appropriate to the ends. The family created by the cross has the global, godly and glorious

---

3. G. R. Dunstan, 'The Marriage Covenant', *Theology*, 78 (1975), pp. 244–52.
4. Lewis Smedes, *Mere Morality*, p. 89.

characteristics that human families were to have created in God's family.

This family exists as a reality now but will be fully experienced only in the future. It contains models of relationship which will be completed in the future. These models can inspire earthly families to become more open, to be more godly and to reflect God's glory. When they do that, they contribute to the creation of God's family. They bring something of the future into the present.

This model is not remote theory. It addresses the central issue facing families today, which is: how can they reduce the emotional pain experienced at home? This pain occurs when social pressures and moral values interlock with harmful rules passed down the generations. Social, psychological and moral forces combine to produce a pot-pourri of hurtful actions, hurtful words and hurtful silences.

The Bible's future-first model can create an 'atmosphere' which will give these families more capacity to change, which will provide them with a moral framework for change, and which will help their response to social injustice to change. It will bring liberation to families in distress.

As such it takes the sacramental model further. By showing how the future impacts on families, it suggests a way in which God's love can be poured into homes: confrontation between the future and the present becomes a channel of grace. It also builds a strong dynamic into the covenant model: its emphasis on change makes it easier for families to change.

Issues on the agenda

One of the difficulties in writing about the family is that the subject is vast. There are so many issues which are a matter of debate. We have dealt with some, touched on others and ignored a good many! To see how far the future-first model is relevant to these issues, I shall list the more important ones and sketch – in just a few lines – the insights that the model might bring to them. It will be an agenda for further thought.

The right to conceive. The model provides an insight into why infertility is so poignant. It reminds us that procreation was an important part of God's plan for families – it was one of the ways they were to create God's family. So we can

ANOTHER VIEW OF FAMILY

acknowledge that it is appropriate for couples to feel anguish in a situation that was not what God intended.

But the model also reminds us that family is a calling. Couples are to marry because they feel called to help build God's family. The same, perhaps, applies to having children. So artificial means of reproduction will not be used simply because a mother *wants* to conceive. That desire may reflect the God-given joy she should have through parenting, but it may also stem from all kinds of selfish motives – her need to feel that she has arrived as an adult for example. Artificial means of conception will be used – if at all – by parents who feel called to have children for the sake of God's family.

The model says nothing about the morality of the various techniques involved.

The right to be born. Nor does the model tell us when a foetus becomes a person. What it does is to remind us that if a foetus is at some stage no more than a potential person, it is still a person with the potential to contribute to God's family.

A mother who identifies with God's family will not ask for an abortion because she thinks she is entitled to one – that smacks of the 'self-please' ethic. If the abortion is justified at all, it will be because the harm done to God's family by having the child is likely to outweigh the child's contribution to that family. But in most cases is that a judgement that human beings are in a position to make? And if not, how many abortions can be justified?

The rights of the child. Many have wanted to affirm the rights of children. But we have noted that this often reflects a self-please morality, and that this ethic encourages a tolerance which may, in practice, neglect the child. The future-first model protects children by providing a framework of proper parenting, which includes encouraging the child to separate from his parents.

The right to be single. The future-first model leans heavily against our society's preoccupation with marriage. It makes singleness as valid a calling as marriage. It shows how from the standpoint of God's family (which reaches into eternity), earthly marriages will be seen as the exception rather than the rule – 'there is no marrying in heaven'.

It puts a strong emphasis on parent–child relationships. More is said about them than marriage, because they are more important. Good marriages (and good singleness) are based on good parenting. It calls on nuclear families to create community in which single people are at home. It is a model for single people, as well as for marrieds.

The right to an alternative marriage. These alternatives range from cohabitation, to sexually open marriages, to serial marriages, to gay marriages. Often those involved deny the value of sexual exclusiveness because they are pessimistic about the future; present desires are more real.

The future-first model challenges that pessimism by highlighting the permanency of God's family; it will outlast all human relationships. The model encourages life-long commitment to one person for the sake of this family. Partners need the security of that commitment to heal past hurts and bring out the best in each other. Only then will they be able to make their fullest contribution to God's family.

Nowhere does Scripture explicitly endorse the notion of gay marriages. Among a variety of biblical insights relevant to the issue, the future-first model challenges the motivation for gay marriages, as for any marriage. It is not enough for gay couples to marry for motives stemming from our society's preoccupation with marriage, or because they think they have the right to marry. Marriage is not to be undertaken purely to satisfy desires and meet rights: it is also a calling for the sake of God's family.

The model of the Father as the perfect parent, combining in himself both so-called 'masculine' and 'feminine' traits, may point to the desirability of parents combining in themselves a rough balance of 'masculine' and 'feminine' qualities. Without suggesting that these traits are the exclusive possession of either sex, is it likely that the balance will be harder to achieve when the couple are both men or both women?

The rights of women. The future-first model sides with women who are opposed to male dominance. In God's family 'masculine' characteristics are not pre-eminent, they are combined equally within the Father and the Son. The Son (who reveals what the Father is like) is both ruler of the world, and the one who gave up his 'masculine' authority to submit – in a 'feminine' way – to the cross. It seems from some of Jesus' teaching that women and men will relate in heaven on the basis of equality.

Old Testament marriages were to pull away from the male-dominated culture of the day and create relationships which strained toward equality; had they achieved this, they would have begun to build a society more akin to what God had in mind. The New Testament teaches that partners are not to do this by asserting rights, as do many feminists. They are to bring out the best in each other through mutual submission.

The right to divorce. The model does not comment directly on when divorce and remarriage are legitimate. But it makes divorce less likely by presenting marriage as a call; couples are not to drift into marriage and then separate when it doesn't work. Submitting to each other's interests will breed greater commitment. Building community will root marriages in a network of support.

The rights of the elderly. The future-first model protects the interests of those who are aging. In God's family the Son will hand back the Kingdom to his Father. Children do much the same when they hand back to their aging parents a little of what they received from them. The extended nature of God's family challenges families to be open to the needs of elderly relatives who have no one to look after them.

The rights of the extended family. The model does not define family in a particular way. It does not say that the family ought to have a nuclear form, or an extended form, or some other form. 'Family' in the Bible can refer to the smallest (nuclear-type) unit, to the clan, to the tribe, to the nation, or to the international gathering in heaven.

What the model does is to challenge families, whatever their form, to be open to outsiders. They are not to close their doors to the world, like many 'privatised' families do today. They are to join with other families to build community – a community which has the feel of an extended family. They are to be concerned for relatives with no one to care for them. But they are to understand that family solidarity reaches beyond these biological ties. It extends to those outside one's kith and kin.

The right to government support. The family nature of the Kingdom challenges governments to create earthly 'kingdoms' with a similar, family character. In that way they will bring part of the future into the present. Without denying the role of other institutions, our model suggests that families have an important part to play in this. The task of creating the global family – in Genesis 1 – 2 – was given to a family. It remained with families in Israel. In the early church, families did much to promote the Kingdom. 'If anything is real', G. K. Chesterton once said, 'it must be local.'

Government today, therefore, should encourage families in their task of building community. For it is as family-style communities are built on the base of society that society itself will be significantly changed. That should be a priority for government because creating a family-like society is a priority for God. Ideally perhaps, government initiatives should be accompanied by an 'impact statement' describing their likely effects on families.

We could add other items on to the agenda, but it is already long enough! Each item bristles with difficulty. Perhaps there are sufficient 'thought-starters', however, to suggest that the future-first model contains pastoral and moral insights relevant to the major issues facing families today. In some cases the insights are of crucial importance.

Families in the world

It is well-known that children who are deprived of security, who are manipulated, who become shuttlecocks in marital war, and whose confidence is undermined by the hurt of parental neglect, will be more prone to juvenile crime, alcoholism and drug abuse. One Swedish study showed that the number of children of divorced parents who had to be admitted to reform schooling was four times as high as for the general population. Another found that forty-two per cent of delinquent boys had divorced parents, against thirteen per cent for the population as a whole. What happens at home affects society.[5]

That is why justice behind the front door will encourage justice outside it. The child who has been instilled with a sense of fairness at home will carry that fairness into the world. The child who has seen her parents handle conflict openly with mutual respect, will avoid manipulation as an adult. The man who felt put down by his parents but has been overwhelmed by the affirmation of his wife, will be less inclined to get even with people at work. Families committed to communities of equality, solidarity and liberty will be concerned about those

---

5. Christian Schumacher, *To Live and Work: A Theological Interpretation.* London 1987, p. 207.

values in the wider society. Domestic fairness is not just for families: it is for the world.

The Bible has a vision that challenges us to be committed to the family, not to any old family, but to human families shaped by God's family. As families are captivated by that family, they will bring a taste of it from heaven to earth. They will leave behind the moribund past, which traps them in hurtful and unfair patterns of behaviour, and they will strain toward the future where all things will be new and where all tears will be wiped away. 'We are here on earth', Pope John XXIII once said, 'not to guard a museum (or a mausoleum!), but to cultivate a garden flourishing with life and promised to a glorious future.' Families are to raise their sights – from home to home.

Bibliography

ABBOTT, WALTER M. (ed.), *The Documents of Vatican II*. London 1967.

ANDERSON, DIGBY & DAWSON, GRAHAM (eds.), *Family Portraits*. Social Affairs Unit, London 1986.

ANDERSON, HERBERT, *The Family and Pastoral Care*. Philadelphia 1984.

ATKINSON, DAVID, *To Have and To Hold. The Marriage Covenant and the Discipline of Divorce*. London 1979.

ATTFIELD, D. G., 'Can God be crucified? A discussion of J. Moltmann', *Scottish Journal of Theology*, 30 (1977), pp. 47–57.

BAILEY, D. S., *The Mystery of Love and Marriage: A Study in the Theology of Sexual Relation*. London 1952.

BAILEY, KENNETH E., *The Cross and the Prodigal*. St Louis 1973.

BALDWIN, JOYCE G., *Haggai, Zechariah, Malachi. An Introduction and Commentary*. Leicester 1972.

BANKS, ROBERT, *Paul's Idea of Community*. Paternoster, Exeter 1980.

BARRETT, C. K., *A Commentary on the First Epistle to the Corinthians*. London 1971.

BARTH, MARKUS, *Ephesians 4–6, A New Translation with Introduction and Commentary*. New York 1974.

BEELS, C. CHRISTIAN & FERBER, ANDREW, 'Family Therapy: A View', *Family Process*, 8 (1969), pp. 280–318.

BENTOVIM, ARNOLD, BARNES, GILL GORELL, COOKLIN, ALAN, *Family Therapy: Complementary Frameworks of Theory and Practice*, vol. 1, London 1982.

BERESFORD, PETER et al., *In Care in North Battersea*. University of Surrey, Guildford 1985.

BERGER, BRIGITTE & PETER L., *The War over the Family: Capturing the Middle Ground*. London 1983.

BERGER, PETER L. & NEUHAUS, RICHARD JOHN, *To Empower People: The Role of Mediating Structures in Public Policy*. Washington 1977.

BLIXON, KAREN, *On Modern Marriage and Other Observations*. Fourth Estate, London 1987.

BIBLIOGRAPHY

BOLBY, JOHN, 'The study and reduction of group tensions in the family', in WALROND-SKINNER, SUE (ed.), *Developments in Family Therapy: Theories and Applications since 1948*. London 1981, pp. 9–15.

BOSZORMENYI-NAGY, IVAN & SPARK, GERALDINE M., *Invisible Loyalties, Reciprocity in Intergenerational Family Therapy*. New York 1973.

BRECHER, ROBERT, 'Karl Barth: Wittgensteinian Theologian Manque', *The Heythrop Journal*, 24 (1983), pp. 290–300.

BROWN, RAYMOND E., DONFRIED, KARL P., FITZMYER, JOSEPH A., REUMANN, JOHN, *Mary in the New Testament*. Philadelphia 1978.

CAMPBELL, BEATRIX, 'Sex – A Family Affair', in SEGAL, LYNNE (ed.), *What is to be done about the family?* London 1983, pp. 157–67.

CHILDS, B. S., *Exodus. A Commentary*. SCM, London 1974.

CLARE, ANTHONY, *Psychiatry in Dissent: Controversial Issues in Thought and Practice*. London 1976.

CLARK, C. A. & WORTHINGTON, E. L., 'Family Variables Affecting the Transmission of Religious Values from Parents to Adolescents: A Review'. *Family Perspective*, vol. 21, no. 1, pp. 1–12.

CLARK, STEPHEN B., *Man and Woman in Christ. An Examination of the Roles of Men and Women in Light of Scripture and the Social Sciences*. Michigan 1980.

CLARK, WENDY, 'Home Thoughts from Not So Far Away: A Personal Look at Family', in SEGAL, LYNNE (ed.), *What is to be done about the family?* London 1983, pp. 168–89.

CLOUSER, ROY, 'Religious Language: A New Look at an Old Problem', paper distributed by the Association for the Advancement of Christian Scholarship, Toronto, 1980.

COOPER, DAVID, *The Death of the Family*. London 1971.

CRAIGIE, P. C., *The Book of Deuteronomy*. Grand Rapids 1976.

CRANFIELD, C. E. B., *The Gospel According to Saint Mark*. Cambridge 1958.

CRANFIELD, C. E. B., 'Thoughts on New Testament Eschatology', *Scottish Journal of Theology*, 35 (1982), pp. 497–512.

DE SATGE, JOHN, *Mary and the Christian Gospel*. London 1976.

DE VAUX, ROLAND, *Ancient Israel: Its Life and Institutions*, London 1961.

DE WAAL, ESTHER, 'Changing Anglican Attitudes towards the Family', *Crucible*, July-Sept. 1982, pp. 106–13.

DOMINIAN, JACK, *Marriage, Faith and Love*. DLT, London 1981.

DUNSTAN, G. R., *The Family is not Broken*. London 1962.

DUNSTAN, G. R., 'The Marriage Covenant', *Theology*, 78 (1975), pp. 244–52.

ELLUL, JACQUES, *The Meaning of the City*. Eerdmans, Grand Rapids 1970.
EVANS, MARY J., *Woman in the Bible*. Exeter 1983.
FIELD, DAVID, 'The divorce debate – Where are we now?', *Themelios*, 8 (1983), pp. 26–31.
FLETCHER, RONALD, *The Family and Marriage in Britain*. London 1966.
GARCIA, JO & MAITLAND, SARA, *Walking on the Water: Women Talk about Spirituality*. Virago Press, London 1983.
GARLAND, DAVID E., 'The Christian's Posture Toward Marriage and Celibacy: 1 Corinthians 7', *Review and Expositor*, 80 (1983), pp. 351–62.
GITTINGS, DIANA, *The Family in Question: Changing Households and Familiar Ideologies*. Macmillan, London 1985.
GOERGEN, DONALD, *The Sexual Celibate*. Seabury Press, New York 1974.
GREENFIELD, GUY, 'Paul and the Eschatological Marriage', *South Western Journal of Theology*, 8 (1982), pp. 33–48.
GREENSTEIN, EDWARD L., 'The Riddle of Samson', *Prooftexts*, 1 (1981), pp. 237–60.
HAMERTON-KELLY, ROBERT, *God the Father: Theology and Patriarchy in the Teaching of Jesus*. Philadelphia 1979.
HARRIS, C. C., *The Family and Industrial Society*. London 1983.
HAUERWAS, STANLEY, *A Community of Character: Toward a Constructive Christian Social Ethic*. Notre Dame 1981.
HAYTER, MARY, *The New Eve in Christ*. SPCK, London 1987.
HENWOOD, MELANIE et al., *Inside the Family: Changing Roles of Men and Women*. Family Policy Studies Centre, London 1987.
HILLERS, DELBERT R., *Covenant: The History of a Biblical Idea*. Baltimore 1969.
HOSKYNS, E. C. & DAVEY, NOEL, *Crucifixion – Resurrection: The Pattern of the Theology and Ethics of the New Testament*. London 1981.
JEREMIAS, JOACHIM, *New Testament Theology*. London 1971.
JEREMIAS, JOACHIM, *The Prayers of Jesus*. London 1967.
JEWETT, P. K., *Man as Male and Female*. Grand Rapids 1975.
KAISER, WALTER C. Jr, *Toward Old Testament Ethics*. Grand Rapids 1983.
KANFER, H. & GOLDSTEIN, ARNOLD P. (eds.), *Helping People Change: A Textbook of Methods*. Oxford 1980.
KELLY, J. N. D., *The Epistles of Peter and Jude*. London 1969.
KNIGHT, GEORGE, A. F., *A Christian Theology of the Old Testament*. London 1959.
KOVEY, JOEL, *A Complete Guide to Therapy: From Psychoanalysis to Behaviour Modification*. London 1981.
KUMAR, KRISHAN, 'The social culture of work: Work, employ-

ment and unemployment as ways of life', *New Universities Quarterly*, 34 (1979/80), pp. 5–28.
LAING, R. D. 'Intervention in Social Situations', in WALROND-SKINNER, SUE (ed.), *Developments in Family Therapy: Theories and Applications since 1948*. London 1981, pp. 9–15.
LAING, R. D., *The Divided Self: An Existential Study in Sanity and Madness*. London 1965.
LAING, R. D., *The Politics of the Family*. Harmondsworth 1976.
LAING, R. D. & ESTERSON, A., *Sanity, Madness and the Family*. London 1970.
LASLETT, PETER & WALL, RICHARD (eds.), *Household and Family in Past Time*. Cambridge 1972.
LEACH, EDMUND, *A Runaway World?* London 1968.
LEWIS, JERRY M., BEAVERS, W. ROBERT, COSSETT, JOHN T., PHILLIPS, VIRGINIA AUSTIN, *No Single Thread: Psychological Health in Family Systems*. New York 1976.
McCONVILLE, J. G. M., *Law and Theology in Deuteronomy*. Sheffield 1984.
MANSFIELD, PENNY, *Young People and Marriage*. Scottish Marriage Council, Edinburgh 1985.
'Marriage' in RAHNER, KARL with ERNST, CORNELIUS & SMYTHE, KEVIN, *Sacramentum Mundi: An Encyclopedia of Theology*, vol. 3, London 1969, pp. 414–8.
MARSHAL I. HOWARD, *Commentary on Luke*. Grand Rapids 1979.
MASON, MIKE, *The Mystery of Marriage*. MARC Europe, Portland 1985.
MAURICE, F. D., *The Kingdom of Christ or Hints to a Quaker Respecting the Principles, Constitution, and Ordinances of the Catholic Church*, vol. 1. London 1958.
MAYERS, A. D. H., *Deuteronomy*. London 1979.
METZ, JOHANNES-BAPTIST & SCHILLEBEECKX, EDWARD (eds.), *God as Father*. New York 1981.
MINEAR, PAUL S., *Images of the Church in the New Testament*. London 1960.
MINUCHIN, SALVADOR, *Families and Family Therapy*. London 1977.
MITMAN, JOHN L. C., *Pre-Marital Counselling: A Manual for Clergy and Counsellors*. New York 1980.
MOBERLY, ELIZABETH R., *Suffering, Innocent and Guilty*. London 1978.
MOISER, JEREMY, 'A reassessment of Paul's view of marriage with reference to 1 Cor. 7', *Journal for the Study of the New Testament*, 18 (1983), pp. 103–22.
MOLTMANN, JURGEN, *The Experiment Hope*. Philadelphia 1975.
MOLTMANN, JURGEN, *The Crucified God*. London 1974.

MOLTMANN, JURGEN, *The Open Church: Invitation to a Messianic Lifestyle*. London 1978.
MOLTMANN, JURGEN, *The Theology of Hope*. New York 1967.
MOLTMANN, JURGEN, *The Trinity and the Kingdom of God: The Doctrine of God*. London 1981.
MOLTMANN-WENDEL, ELISABETH, *A Land Flowing with Milk and Honey: Perspectives on Feminist Theology*. SCM, London 1986.
MORGAN, D. H. J., *Social Theory and the Family*. London 1975.
MORRIS, LEON, *The Cross in the New Testament*. Exeter 1967.
MORSE, CHRISTOPHER, *The Logic of Promise in Moltmann's Theology*. Philadelphia 1979.
MOUNT, FERDINAND, *The Subversive Family: A History of Love and Marriage*. London 1982.
MURDOCH, GEORGE P., *Culture and Society*. Pittsburgh 1965.
NATIONAL MARRIAGE GUIDANCE COUNCIL, *Change in Marriage*. London 1982.
NATIONAL MARRIAGE GUIDANCE COUNCIL, *Relating to Marriage*. London 1985.
NAVA, MICA, 'From Utopian to Scientific Feminism?', in SEGAL, LYNNE, (ed.) *What is to be done about the family?* London 1983, pp. 65–105.
NICHOLS, A. et al., *Transforming Families and Communities*. London 1987.
NIDITCH, SUSAN, 'The "Sodomite" Theme in Judges 19–20. Family, Community, and Social Disintegration', *Catholic Biblical Quarterly*, 44 (1982), pp. 365–78.
NOTH, MARTIN, *Exodus. A Commentary*. London 1962.
ODDIE, WILLIAM, *What Will Happen to God? Feminism and the Reconstruction of Christian Belief*. London 1984.
OPEN UNIVERSITY (Changing Experience of Women Course Team – eds.), *The Changing Experience of Women*. Oxford 1982.
OPEN UNIVERSITY (School and Society Course Team – eds.), *School and Society*. London 1971.
OPPENHEIMER, HELEN, *Law and Love*. London 1962.
PANNENBERG, WOLFHART, *Jesus – God and Man*. London 1968.
PEDERSON, JOHS, *Israel: Its Life and Culture*. OUP, London 1926.
POSTER, MARK, *Critical Theory of the Family*. London 1978.
RAHNER, KARL with ERNST, CORNELIUS & SMYTHE, KEVIN, 'Marriage' in *Sacramentum Mundi: An Encyclopedia of Theology*, vol. 3, London 1969 pp. 414–8.
RAMSEY, IAN T., *Religious Language*. SCM, London 1957.
RAPOPORT, R. N., FOGARTY, M. P., RAPOPORT, R. (eds.), *Families in Britain*. London 1982.
RAPOPORT, RHONDA & ROBERT N., & STRELITZ, ZIONA, *Fathers, Mothers and Others: Towards New Alliances*. London 1977.

READ, D. H. C., 'The Cry of Dereliction', *Expository Times*, 68 (1957–8), pp. 260–2.

RIMMER, LESLEY, *Families in Focus: Marriage, Divorce and Family Patterns*. London 1981.

ROBINSON, H. WHEELER, *Corporate Personality in Ancient Israel*. Edinburgh 1981.

ROBINSON, J. ARMITAGE, *St Paul's Epistle to the Ephesians, with Exposition and Notes*. London 1903.

RUETHER, ROSEMARY, 'An unrealized revolution. Searching Scripture for a model of the family'. *Christianity and Crisis*, 43 (1983), pp. 399–404.

RYDER, JUDITH, & SILVER, HAROLD, *Modern English Society: History and Structure, 1850–1970*. London 1970.

SCHILLEBEECKX, EDWARD, *Marriage. Human Reality and Saving Mystery*. London 1965.

SCHLUTER, M. & CLEMENTS, R., *Reactivating the Extended Family, From Biblical Norms to Public Policy*. Cambridge 1986.

SECCOMBE, W., 'The housewife and her labour under capitalism', *New Left Review*, 83 (1974), pp. 3–31.

SIMON, RICHARD, 'Still R. D. Laing after all these years', *Networker*, May-June 1983, pp. 23–61.

SKYNNER, R. & CLEESE, JOHN, *Families and How to Survive Them*. Methuen, London 1984.

SMAIL, THOMAS A., *The Forgotten Father*. London 1980.

SMEDES, LEWIS, *Mere Morality*. Tring 1983.

STAMM, J. J. & ANDREW, M. E., *The Ten Commandments in Recent Research*. London 1967.

STINNETT, NICK, CHESSER, BARBARA, DE FRAIN, JOHN (eds.), *Building Family Strengths: Blueprints for Action*. Nebraska 1979.

TAYLOR, VINCENT, *The Gospel According to St Mark*. London 1952.

THIELICKE, HELMUT, *The Ethics of Sex*. Cambridge 1964.

THOMPSON, E. P., 'Happy Families', *New Society*, 8 Sept. 1977, pp. 499–501.

TRIBLE, PHYLLIS, *God and the Rhetoric of Sexuality*. Philadelphia 1978.

TRIBLE, PHYLLIS, 'Woman in the Old Testament', *The Interpreter's Dictionary of the Bible*, supplementary vol., Nashville, 1976, pp. 962–66.

VANIER, JEAN, *Man and Woman He Made Them*. London 1985.

VON RAD, GERHARD, *Deuteronomy. A Commentary*. London 1966.

VON RAD, GERHARD, *Genesis: A Commentary*. London 1972.

VON RAD, GERHARD, *Old Testament Theology*, vols. 1 & 2, London 1975.

VRIEZEN, Th. C., *An Outline of Old Testament Theology*. Oxford 1962.

WALROND-SKINNER, SUE, *Family Matters: The Pastoral Care of Personal Relationships*. SPCK, London 1988.

WALTER, J. A., *A Long Way From Home: A Sociological Exploration of Contemporary Idolatry*. Exeter 1979.

WHITFIELD, RICHARD, (ed.), *Families Matter: Towards a Programme of Action*. Marshall Pickering, Basingstoke 1987.

WILLMOTT, PETER, *Social Networks, Informal Care and Public Policy*. London 1986.

WOLFF, HANS WALTER, *Anthropology of the Old Testament*. London 1974.

WOLFF, HANS WALTER, 'Problems between the Generations in the Old Testament', in CRENSHAW, JAMES L. & WILLIS, JOHN T. (eds.), *Essays in Old Testament Ethics: J. Phillip Hyatt In Memoriam*. New York 1974.

WRIGHT, CHRISTOPHER J. H., 'The Israelite Household and the Decalogue: The Social Background and Significance of Some Commandments', *Tyndale Bulletin*, 30 (1979), pp. 101–24.

WRIGHT, CHRISTOPHER J. H., *Living as the People of God: The Relevance of Old Testament Ethics*. London 1983.

YOUNG, FRANCES, *Can These Dry Bones Live?* London 1982.

YOUNG, MICHAEL, & WILLMOTT, PETER, *Family and Kinship in East London*. London 1962.

ZARETSKY, ELI, *Capitalism, the Family and Personal Life*. London 1976.